"Haven't you ever wanted to change your life, Lisa? Start again? Do something entirely different than before?"

She stared at Ethan. Was he kidding? That was what brought her to New Beginnings. She honestly wanted to get her life back... and straightened out. She wanted to make a stable home for Cecily and be the kind of mother that won prizes.

Ethan's eyes said she had a willing listener who would be sympathetic. She was tempted. "Can I trust you?" At his frown, she blinked. "Yes, yes, I can. It's just...I can't trust everyone, you know?"

**Books by Ruth Scofield**

Love Inspired

*In God's Own Time* #29
*The Perfect Groom* #65
*Whispers of the Heart* #89
*Wonders of the Heart* #124
*Loving Thy Neighbor* #145
*Take My Hand* #219
*Love Came Unexpectedly* #286
*A Mother's Promise* #337

## *RUTH SCOFIELD*

loves to write about God's love, and His Son, Jesus. Since she does not have a father, she loves to call God, Father, and to feel the faith that that builds. She also loves to play with her grandchildren.

Ruth's first book was published in 1993 just a month after her return to her native Missouri after years in the East. She often sets her novels in Missouri, where there are lakes and hills aplenty, and as many stories and history as people. This is Ruth's eighth Love Inspired novel.

# A MOTHER'S PROMISE

## RUTH SCOFIELD

Steeple
Hill®

Published by Steeple Hill Books™

STEEPLE HILL BOOKS

Steeple
Hill®

ISBN 0-373-81251-5

A MOTHER'S PROMISE

www.SteepleHill.com

**Printed in U.S.A.**

But seek first His kingdom, and His righteousness, and all these things will be given to you as well. Therefore do not worry about tomorrow, for tomorrow will worry about itself. Each day has enough trouble of its own.

—*Matthew* 6:33–34

Do not judge, or you too will be judged. For in the same way you judge others, you will be judged, and with the measure you use, it will be measured to you.

—*Matthew* 7:1–2

To all the young mothers in my family
who give unrestricted devotion and
love to their young.

# Chapter One

Lisa Marley guided the dual-wheel rusty red pickup truck into the deep shadows of the parking lot. A lighted sign declared she had reached the right place—Blue River Valley Community Church.

"Okay, God," she whispered. "Here I am, as promised."

She turned off the growling engine and headlights. A few windows illuminated nearby houses, but there was only silence, and the church stood quietly before her in the autumn mist of early evening.

Silence was good, Lisa thought, only she'd grown unused to it. She shivered. From the cool evening or from nerves, she wondered?

Only a small number of cars were scattered across the parking lot.

Her friend Beth Anne Hostetter had warned her there wouldn't be a large crowd when she'd issued the invitation to New Beginnings. The organization was meant for men and women over forty who needed just what the name implied. A new beginning in life. A second start.

Beth Anne said the person in charge of this ministry, Dr. Michael Faraday, was a very capable, compassionate man, and Lisa could trust him.

Sure, sure… Trust.

Beth Anne knew Lisa's fears. Lisa had faith in very few people these days. Sometimes not even in herself.

Those were the middle-of-the-night times when she lay still, listening to her own heartbeat, begging God to talk to her. To tell her how to get her life back.

Did God hear her? She didn't know, was never sure.

But she'd promised Beth Anne to give New Beginnings a chance, and she was willing to do anything to help rebuild her life.

New Beginnings wasn't just another singles group, Beth Anne insisted. It offered hope for people. Some were in crisis, some in a rut. Others simply needed to change their attitudes toward life.

That certainly described her—Lisa Jane Marley. Beth Anne's passion about a loving God had drawn Lisa to a Bible Study last year, and over the months, Lisa had tentatively given her heart to God. Now she was learning the hard part—trusting Him with every ounce of her being.

Her nerves felt stretched as she contemplated getting out of the truck and walking through that door. What if those people asked questions?

Her stomach tensed. Beth Anne had assured her that no one knew of Lisa's recent history, but still…

If anyone asked Lisa what she'd done this last year or two, or where she'd been, she was outta here.

Yet Beth Anne had said Lisa could make new friends. She couldn't ask for more. Beyond that, the group's ideals appealed to Lisa. It offered her a place to work on her future, with people her own age who had similar needs.

She clenched her eyes shut while a familiar gut-deep yearning and hope rose high. *Please Lord, let this count…*

"Okay, God," she murmured aloud, taking a deep breath to steady herself. "This is it, so You gotta keep Your promise and stay with me. I'm not doing this all alone."

Swiping her hand down her thigh, she opened the door and slid to the ground. As she started across the lot, another car pulled into it. Instinctively, she turned her head toward the new arrival. The high beams hit her face, momentarily blinding her.

Lisa froze. Her heartbeat jumped, then raced. Her lips went dry. For one long moment, she couldn't make herself move.

The car parked, and Lisa blinked. On shaky legs, she ran the last few yards to reach the sidewalk that led to the church door.

"Hey, wait up!"

She ignored the masculine shout and kept walking. Almost at the door, she paused long enough to suck air all the way into her lungs.

"Sorry about that," came a blithe baritone behind her.

Lisa glanced over her shoulder long enough to take in a tall, rather broad-shouldered male flashing her a wide grin. There didn't seem to be a jot of real regret in his shadowed expression.

"Anyone ever tell you it's rude to blast your high beams in a crowd?" she snapped.

"A crowd?" Another car was turning into the lot, but the tarmac was empty of pedestrians. The man fell into step beside her, a scarred guitar case dangling from his grip.

"A place that's often crowded, then."

He reached past her for the door handle. The air between them stirred, and she sidestepped to avoid closer contact, only to bump into the instrument case.

"Sorry," he said again.

"I'll just bet," she muttered under her breath.

"Hello and welcome," greeted a tall, rangy man as Lisa entered the foyer. A touch of silver threaded his thick brown hair, and Lisa guessed him to be in his forties. He was neatly dressed in a casual cotton checked shirt and summer-weight slacks. Clear green eyes met hers with neither flirtation nor judging assessment. "I'm Michael Faraday."

Lisa was about to answer when her companion spoke up enthusiastically.

"Hiya, Mike. How's it going?"

"Hi there, Ethan. It's been a good day." Mike nodded, as though conceding something that was understood between them.

"Glad you remembered the guitar. Jimmy has his, too, so we can open with a little music. Who's your friend?"

"Don't really know, preacher. Found her out in the parking lot looking lost. She just sorta followed me up to the church door."

"I didn't!" Lisa protested, then clamped her mouth closed. He made her sound like a lost puppy looking for a home.

A lot of teeth…she thought as she turned her annoyed gaze on Ethan. His grin widened, his eyes sparkled. Lisa felt a slight flush creep up her face.

He's cute and he knows it! Jerk…

She was here at New Beginnings for a lot of reasons, but flirting wasn't on her agenda.

Forgetting her earlier hesitancy, she offered the minister her hand in greeting. "I'm Lisa Marley."

"Glad to meet you, Lisa." Michael spoke with sincerity. "I hope you'll feel at home with us tonight."

Three other people came into the foyer, and the minister turned to welcome them. "Hi, folks. Go on into the fellowship hall. It'll be roomy enough there."

 hadn't a clue which direction to take,
 fell into step with the others. They

headed down the hall on the left, through double doors opened wide, into a spacious, airy room. At one end, a semi-circle of chairs already held nearly a dozen people, chatting to one another. Off to the side, a man had hooked up an electric guitar and was strumming a few chords.

In the center of the room, a huge Bible lay on a simple oak podium.

"See you later." Ethan left her to join the other musician.

"Uh-huh." Her reply was so noncommittal as to be ungracious, but she wasn't about to encourage the guy. In Lisa's opinion, most men didn't need but a flutter of interest to try a pick-up. Finding guys who wanted her wasn't her problem.

It had never been her problem.

"Lisa!" Beth Anne called her name. Lisa hurried toward her friend, gratitude and relief flooding her.

"I'm only going to remember first names," Beth Anne said as she started introductions. "This is just the third meeting for New Beginnings, you know. Let's see. Jenny, isn't it? And Pam, and Karen and Cindy. The guys are Lorne, Matt, Charlie and Jimmy, helping out on the guitar. And the man you met as you came in—can't recall his name."

"Ethan," Lisa supplied.

"That's it—Ethan Vale," Jenny said. Her blue eyes shone in keen interest. "Can't wait to hear him. He played in a band once upon a time."

"I've heard him," Cindy added. "At a banking function, before his wife Sharon died. The band played bluegrass that night, but Sharon said they also did country-and-western. He's really good."

Obviously, Ethan was already popular among this crowd, Lisa mused. And he was widowed. A thin ribbon of sympathy threaded through her consciousness. She let her gaze roam his way and watched him, tuning his acoustic guitar along with the other musician. He had long, masculine fingers that stroked the strings with care.

Lisa put a clamp on her wayward thoughts. She'd had enough romantic entanglements to last a lifetime, and they'd all been disastrous. Besides, she didn't intend to let anything get in the way of what she had to do now.

The fact Ethan was widowed did tie in with what Beth Anne told her about this group. New Beginnings was made up of all kinds of people, in all phases of life, looking for new directions.

"Didn't know that," Beth Anne remarked, gazing around the room as others drifted in. "Well, I haven't met everyone yet. Looks like our crowd has increased, praise God. You sit tight, Lisa, and I'll join you in a minute."

Lisa exchanged a general greeting with the others, too nervous to offer a smile, and sat down in the second row on the end seat. Michael stepped up to the podium and welcomed them all, waited for the low hum of chatter to quiet, then opened the meeting with prayer. True to her word, Beth Anne slipped silently into the chair next to Lisa, giving Lisa's knee a reassuring pat as she did.

Lisa sighed and let her thoughts join in as Michael's rich, deep voice intoned an earnest praise of God's presence in their lives, their rock in time of trouble, then sought God's attention, help and blessings for them all.

*Yes, Lord. Do You hear him? He's a minister, so I guess You just have to listen to him. And I guess he's first in line for receiving Your help. But I'm here, too, and I'm one of those who needs all the help I can get. I*

*can't afford to mess up again. Oh, by the*
*way, thanks for the job. I can get tips as a*
*waitress. If the court had let me work in a*
*place that served drinks, I'd earn more, but*
*that's okay. I'll work as hard as I need to,*
*You'll see. If only Aunt Katherine will see*
*reason...*

Fifteen minutes later, as the musicians let
the opening music drift to a close, Lisa
conceded that Ethan knew how to use his
guitar. The man could *play.*

So what? Lisa mused. That didn't cover
much by way of character.

She was into character study these
days—good, bad, weak, strong. Her obser-
vations of those around her had become an
obsession.

The meeting covered a lot of ground. There
were announcements of planned activities,
most of them strictly for fun and bonding,
Bible studies held in small groups, and the
private counseling services that Michael offered.

Maybe she should go see him, Lisa
thought. Would Beth Anne go with her?

"We officially launch an ad in two weeks,"
Michael went on, "for our first big event. An
all-day seminar entitled What Are You Doing

for the Rest of Your Life? and subtitled, Following God's Blueprint."

She certainly needed *that*. But it was on a Saturday... Her thoughts drifted; she'd have to work.

"Blueprint?" commented one of the men. "Guess I was standing behind a door when they was passing out them things, 'cause life has sure passed me by."

Chuckles greeted the remark, and another man answered, "Ken, you haven't enough life in you to make a blip on the charts in the first place. Life can't help but pass you by when it can't even find you."

"Then it's an all-fired surety that God's gotta give me something to work with for the next few years, isn't it?" Ken parried, the lines in his face crinkling as he talked. "I've gotta make up for lost time. Maybe it's a good time to ask Cindy here for a date."

Cindy turned toward the man in cut-off jeans, his short brown hair flying every way but straight. Lisa's gaze followed Cindy's carefully narrowed stare.

Ken gave an exaggerated groan.

While those around her laughed, Lisa found herself wanting to smile, too. She could see this crowd liked to tease, but their friendliness included a real compassion. Slowly her muscles relaxed, and she began to enjoy the meeting.

Then Michael regained their attention, explaining who the speakers would be at the seminar, and what they hoped to cover.

"It's a dynamite program, so it's a good time to invite other people to come. We want to serve each other here, folks, while we're finding or expanding our own walk with the Lord. Even though we're a little out of the way here in River's Edge, I don't think people will mind if we can give them what they need. We can still become an effective force for boomers at a crossroads."

"Sounds cool, Michael," Pam said. "What can we do to help set up for the day?"

"We need to get the word out, mostly. And Beth Anne will need some help in taking reservations and organizing the kitchen. We're contracting with Buck's Barbecue for lunch, but we'll still need some set-up and clean-up help."

After that, Michael launched into the serious side of the meeting. He gave a message from Romans, and Lisa stilled her wandering thoughts to concentrate.

"Most of us in this group are reaching for

higher gains now, more than just the material things that topped our list of needs in our twenties and thirties. We've somehow missed the narrow road.

"Those decades have also shown us how vulnerable we are to human mistakes. What the Bible calls sin. We've discovered our own weaknesses and deeper needs, and often we are anxious or depressed, and we're desperate to feel God's love and forgiveness. I'd like to remind you all that loving us is what God does.

"As we wrap up the evening, let's go home with these words from Romans 8:35-39. 'Who shall separate us from the love of Christ? Shall trouble or hardship or persecution or famine or nakedness or danger or sword?

'As it is written, For Your sake we face death all day long; we are considered as sheep to be slaughtered.

'No, in all these things we are more than conquerors through Him who loved us.

'For I am convinced that neither death nor life, neither angels nor demons, nor anything else in all creation, will be able to separate us from the love of God that is in Christ Jesus our Lord.'"

Nothing? Lisa wondered. Not even her sins? The thought was reassuring, as Beth Anne had told her.

But what about this terrible thirst for revenge?

Lisa pushed the thought down, along with all the ugly reasons for feeling that she was unlovable. She clung to the soothing words of love and forgiveness. Perhaps Beth Anne was right about her needing this group.

They adjourned for coffee and refreshments, which were set up toward the back of the room. It was someone's birthday, and Pam had brought a cake. Everyone made a production of singing "Happy Birthday," then the people milled around, talking among themselves.

Lisa glanced at her watch. This was the point at which she wanted to run. She had to be home by ten, anyway. But with Beth Anne's eagle eye on her, she didn't have a chance to slip out unnoticed. When Cindy came up to speak with Beth Anne, Lisa nodded and smiled, then moved to stand at the end of the table.

Ten minutes. Then she'd leave.

"So it's Lisa, huh? What's the last name again?" Lisa turned to see Ethan standing behind her. She noted his brown eyes had warm amber glints, like the amber earrings she'd once owned.

"Marley."

"I'm Ethan Vale." He picked up a foam cup and offered, "Coffee?"

"No, thanks." She glanced at the exit. Five. She'd give it five minutes more.

"You don't drink coffee?"

"Sure. Sometimes."

"But you don't want any now? Actually, I like to watch my caffeine intake, too. Does it keep you awake? I can get you something else."

"No. Um, thank you." Her truck keys made a nice satisfying lump in her denim pocket. If she left now, she'd have time to run by Aunt Katherine's house. Just to look at it. These days, she could come and go at her own choosing—as long as she was home before curfew.

"I think the kitchen has a supply of tea," Ethan said. His inviting gaze urged her to make her request known. "Or lemonade wouldn't bother you. How about some cake?"

"No, thanks."

"Why not? You can't be one of those women always on a diet." His quick glance down her form-fitting jeans held an admiring glint.

"You can't be one of those men who never turns down a sweet," she countered. Everything extra she ate went right to her hips, but she wasn't going to tell him that.

"Aw, come on. It's chocolate."

"So?"

"So, chocolate is one of my favorite vegetables, and I always eat my vegetables."

Yeah, this guy thought he was cute, all right. At least two of the other women thought so, too, from the envious glances tossed her way.

"Thanks, but no thanks," she muttered. "I have to go."

Giving Beth Anne a quick wave, she made a beeline for the double doors.

Ethan followed her. "Hey, I'll walk you to your car."

"You don't have to bother. I'm used to being on my own."

"Really?" He opened the outside door and allowed her to precede him. "No boyfriend?"

"No." The thought of anyone in their age group having "boyfriends" or "girlfriends" seemed ludicrous to her.

Never mind, she thought. Engaging in useless conversation that passed as flirting was another habit she'd given up. Besides, her mind kept jumping ahead. She wanted to race across the parking lot and gun the truck's engine into action. Why had she thought it an advantage to park in the corner space?

"Did you just move here or something?" Ethan asked as they made their way across the lot.

"Yes…no. I, um, just moved to Independence."

"I used to live in Kansas City. In Westport. But now I live here in River's Edge. Hey, want to do a movie on Saturday?"

Lisa climbed into the truck and held her breath as she turned the key in the ignition. She sighed in relief when the engine started. Uncle Fred insisted the truck ran like a top, in spite of the body rust.

Would Aunt Katherine allow her in the house at this hour?

"So how about it?" Ethan's tone cut into her thoughts.

"Um…can't. Have to go, really. Nice meeting you, Ethan."

"Okay. See you next Thursday."

"Sure, sure…."

Maybe.

## Chapter Two

Katherine Barge, the woman Lisa had called "aunt" all her life, was really her mother's cousin. She and her husband, Mark, lived in a forty-year-old ranch-style house in Kansas City. They'd been the only ones Lisa's mother, Betty, could turn to for any kind of help during Lisa's troubled youth, and they'd grudgingly given Lisa a home for a while. But Katherine's help always carried a heavy dose of look-at-all-I've-done-for-you grievances and warnings of dire consequences to pay if Betty didn't find some backbone to cope with life.

Her mother never had, Lisa admitted.

Then it became "if Lisa doesn't mend her ways…" Katherine also berated Betty's weakness when it came to disciplining her daughter.

Katherine enumerated Betty's failings over supper almost every night. If Betty hadn't chosen to marry that no-good lowlife, Rick—against her very sound advice, Katherine usually included—then she wouldn't find herself in such a bind now. If Betty had stood up to that bully, she wouldn't have sustained the black eyes or broken arms or been abandoned. If Betty would only snap out of this so-called depression and get a job, then she could make it on her own.

Katherine's list stretched to include Lisa. Her teenage transgressions piled higher as the months dragged out. She didn't clean the kitchen properly. Her skirts and her shorts were too short, her hair was worn too wild. She took forever at her homework, keeping the household up late. And if she continued to hang out with that crazy wild kid down the street, she'd find trouble.

What Katherine complained of most was the way the boys looked at Lisa.

Lisa's answer was to make herself less and less visible at home and to find attention elsewhere. When the boys found her attractive, she responded with a slow sexy smile she'd learned from the movies.

Eventually, Lisa and her mom found an

apartment of their own, but life did not improve. With her mother's spotty work record and frequent inability to cope, Lisa grew up fast. She learned to juggle their income and bills, her schoolwork, her after-school job, the household and her mom—until Betty finally remarried and moved to Florida.

At seventeen, Lisa had been on her own. Emotionally, she still was on her own, she thought now as she waited at Aunt Katherine's door. On her own again except for the assurance that the Lord was with her. But that was so new…she didn't really know…

The front door opened a crack. Katherine's lined face hardened the moment she spotted Lisa. "Oh. It's you. Might've known."

Lisa despised the fact she'd fulfilled every horrible prediction Aunt Katherine had hurled at her over the years. She had no excuses, but she'd worked diligently to turn her life around this past year.

Behind Katherine, the TV spouted the nightly news and weather. The predicted cold front already made the temperature feel icy. They'd lost the last remnant of summer, Lisa guessed. Like her. She had nothing of her youth left, and only one bright star in her future.

"Yeah, it's me."

"What are you doing here at this time of night, Lisa? Past your curfew? I'm about ready for bed."

"You know why…"

"Who is it, Kate?" Uncle Mark called as he came from the back of the house.

Lisa's fingers tightened on her shoulder purse as she held Katherine's severe gaze. "May I come in, Aunt Katherine?"

"She's asleep," Katherine snapped. "You can't disturb her."

"I won't, I promise. I'll only look at her."

"You're outside your visiting hours, girl. You weren't supposed to come until Sunday."

"I know that. Please?" Lisa despised begging, but swallowed her pride. She'd be on her knees if it would help her cause. "Please, Aunt Katherine. I can't wait till Sunday. It's been months—"

"Let her in, Kate." Mark's commanding tone had an underlying note of compassion.

Lisa held her breath. She didn't dare acknowledge Mark's help.

Katherine's lips thinned, but after flashing Mark an enraged glare, she swung the door wide. "All right. But only for a minute, y'hear? If you make any trouble, then don't expect to come here on Sunday. Now don't you dare wake the child. She's got nursery school in the morning."

"She does?" Lisa stepped inside, so eager that she barely kept herself from racing to the tiny back bedroom where she'd stayed with her mother. "Oh. I didn't know...you didn't tell me..."

The house smelled the same—of strong disinfectant and furniture polish. A fast glimpse of the hall bathroom as she passed showed the same bowl of plastic flowers she remembered on the vanity. Only a foam ball on the floor indicated a change in her aunt's routine.

Katherine followed close on her heels, still hissing a protest. "This isn't wise, Lisa. If Mrs. Braddock hears about this..."

Mention of her parole officer was a threat Lisa expected.

"Mrs. Braddock would understand." She hoped. "She has grandchildren..."

Tiptoeing, Lisa crept to the side of the white daybed that had replaced the old double bed she recalled. A small form barely raised the blanket.

Her breathing grew shallow as she gazed at her daughter. Cecily lay on her side, her tiny palm under her cheek, her mouth pink and sweetly bowed. Light-brown curls covered the little girl's head, and Lisa tentatively brushed them with a butterfly touch. She yearned to hold her, to kiss those plump cheeks. To hear the music of her giggles and sing the duck song Cecily had loved just before they were parted.

What was her favorite song now? Did she still hate carrots? She'd grown, Lisa realized. Her limbs were longer. How tall was she now? Could she skip? Lisa could remember her little girl trying to get both feet to cooperate.

Had she forgotten her mother?

"Hi, baby," she whispered, stroking one tiny hand.

Fierce possessiveness gripped Lisa's heart, while silent tears gathered. She didn't even try to stop their slide down her cheeks. Cecily was her one bright star. Lisa would do whatever she had to to get her daughter back. To protect her…

"Mommy's here. I came to see you as soon as I could." She was three years old, yet Cecily's skin still felt baby-soft.

"Your five minutes are up," Katherine said.

Lisa continued to gaze at her daughter. Hers. Not Katherine's.

Not Rudy's, either, in spite of the biological truth. But saddling Cecily with that knowledge wasn't in Lisa's plans. Getting involved with Rudy was *her* sin, not her daughter's, and she'd paid dearly with humiliation and total disillusionment. At her age, too, when it was expected she'd have gained some smarts. She'd been so *stupid*.

Only her acceptance of God's forgiveness had restored anything left of hope for her.

Lisa couldn't lay the piece of garbage that Rudy was on Cecily and expect her to grow up whole, and with any self-confidence. Lisa had suffered that kind of childhood—she wouldn't inflict it on her own daughter. And Rudy didn't want them, a truth that had come down on her like an ancient burial stone at the time.

Oddly enough, she now thanked God for Rudy's disinterest. Growing up without a father wasn't the worst of sins, as she knew. Plenty of kids were raised by only one parent. She was ready to accept that the blame and blessing of Cecily's birth was hers alone.

Only a few months ago, while in Beth

Anne's company, Lisa had vowed to God that if He'd only help her to be free of her past, she'd be the best mother to Cecily she could. She'd live her life on that narrow, sin-free path that the Bible described could be hers through Jesus, and she would teach Cecily His ways.

Now she had to prove it. To the courts. To Aunt Katherine. To herself. And to God, if she expected Him to help her.

"That's enough," Katherine hissed, hauling Lisa's dreams out of the clouds. The older woman's fingers pinched her upper arm, urging her from the room.

Giving Cecily one last glance, Lisa bit her lip. Every cell in her body protested leaving Cecily, but if she hoped to win back the right to raise her child, she had to cooperate now. She'd already pushed her luck for tonight.

"Thank you," she murmured past the emotion that clogged her throat. She moved slowly out of the tiny bedroom and down the hall toward the living room.

"You should be grateful," Aunt Katherine said with a sniff. "You're lucky we've agreed to care for Cecily."

"I am, Aunt Katherine. Really." At least she knew where Cecily was, and that the child was safe and well looked after. Some of the women she'd met while serving her sentence had children in foster homes and no hope of getting them back.

"Humph… With your irresponsible behavior, I'm surprised the court didn't step in and take her away from you altogether. And if you start that wild life—"

"That's in the past, Aunt Katherine. I've changed. I'm working hard, taking all the overtime I can get at the restaurant to save money, and keeping my nose clean. Soon I'll have enough to make a home for Cecily again. Uncle Fred can tell you."

"Oh, Fred." Katherine made a brushing motion as if to rid herself of a disgusting piece of lint. "What does he know? He's just like your mother, good for nothing but partying on a Saturday night. A weak, sorry excuse of a man."

"Well, that's not—" Lisa caught herself. Arguing with Aunt Katherine would only antagonize her further. And there was a glimmer of truth in the accusations. But at least Uncle Fred had offered Lisa a place to live in his tiny ramshackle house until she could get on her feet. Until she could make a home for Cecily again. "Uncle Fred's okay."

"Still rebellious, aren't you?"

"No, really… I have changed. I won't make any more stupid moves."

"Humph! Your coming here tonight doesn't exactly show intelligence, now does it? And you're out running the roads past your curfew. That hasn't changed."

"I couldn't help myself this time, Aunt Katherine. I had to see Cecily. I'm leaving now. I'll go straight home, I promise. I'll be home in twenty minutes."

"Yeah, well, I've heard that one before. Excuses, always excuses. From your mother and from you. Your mother couldn't hold a job because she was always sick. You—you're so smart that you got yourself mixed up with a married man who gave you a child, and then landed you in jail. What kind of a mother is that for Cecily? One that breaks the law! I have half a mind to call Mrs. Braddock."

Almost out of the door, Lisa turned abruptly. She'd been home for less than a week and didn't know her parole officer that well. "Please, Aunt Katherine…"

Catching a glimpse of triumph in Katherine's gaze, she felt her stomach sink. Begging didn't always help, she'd discovered.

Lisa straightened her back and lifted her

chin. She was through with begging—from anyone. She was through taking any more guff, too. She was the first to admit she'd made some half-witted mistakes in judging the men in her life, but that was in the past. Beth Anne had assured her that the Lord's forgiveness and grace was there for her, it was for anyone—a promise she clung to as her lifeline out of a hellish situation.

"You won't have to, Aunt Katherine," she said, determined to tell the unvarnished truth whenever it was called for, and take any knocks that came her way. "Because I'll tell her about this myself. I'm due to see her tomorrow, and I'll explain about coming."

Katherine's blue eyes glinted like granite. "You'd better get rid of that chip you carry on your shoulder, my girl, or you won't have any friends left to listen to you whine. And you just may lose your rights to see Cecily again until the child is grown."

This time, Katherine's threat held a bite. Her heart in her throat, Lisa took half a step forward, facing the other woman toe to toe. "What do you mean?"

"I mean I've consulted a lawyer about adopting Cecily."

"You can't do that, Aunt Katherine! I don't intend to give Cecily up."

"You're an unfit mother! I think that will speak in the court system."

Lisa gritted her teeth to prevent herself from saying something she'd regret. "I never once neglected Cecily, ever," she said at last. "I made some bad choices about…about her father, that's true, but I thought— Never mind. I love Cecily with my last breath. I won't sign any such papers."

"That still might not affect what a judge decides," Katherine warned, a gleeful note in her voice.

"My life is different now." Lisa prayed her fear wouldn't rob her of determination to put her old ways behind her. She *had* changed, but she hadn't had much time on her side to prove it. "Any judge will take that into account."

"We'll see, won't we? We'll just see."

Those words resounded in Lisa's ears all the way home. A threat. Rage and a sense of betrayal made her seethe. What a hard case Aunt Katherine could be. Well, she'd show her…she'd show everybody.

But in her own way, at least Aunt Katherine cared about Cecily. She would take good care of her.

Lisa shook her head to dispel her irritations. To get her daughter back, she had to look out for herself, to plan and save, to be prepared and strong. Not like before.

Lord have mercy, she'd been so gullible... At her age, too. She'd been long past the time in life when one could label such dewy-eyed trust as youthful foolishness.

Never again.

If only she could find Rudy, that double-dealing, lying two-headed snake. If she could track him down, she'd personally throttle him until his face went purple. Then she'd kick him until he couldn't sit and truss him up like a prize deer, tie him atop the truck, and parade him all the way to the police department.

She nosed the old truck onto the gravel space that Uncle Fred used as a parking spot, picturing how silly and satisfying such a sight would be. She even felt a chuckle bubbling up at the thought. Then she sighed. Beth Anne and everyone else would say she should let the police handle Rudy. Or point out the Lord's directive, "Revenge is mine..."

"I can't do that just yet, Lord," she

muttered aloud. "I have to know that skunk is going to pay for what he's done."

If she ever got Rudy in her sights again, she'd go after him with everything she had in her power, and she didn't envision a pretty outcome. Over the last twenty months, a number of delightful ideas had come her way. Dumping a bucket of red paint all over him as he slept was a favorite. Or hot tar…yeah, she liked that old-fashioned way of dealing with deceivers. Tar and feathers. She'd use an old feather boa or two, bright red…

What would really please her would be to see him prosecuted for his embezzlement, as *she* had been. But as far as she knew, he was sunning himself alongside his "poor, dying wife" somewhere on a Caribbean beach, untouchable.

Uncle Fred, white-haired and paunchy, lay sprawled across the couch listening to the late news, when she entered the small cottage-style house. The phone rang as she closed the door.

"It's for you, Lisa." Uncle Fred yawned widely and handed her the old-fashioned rotary phone.

"Oh? Who is it?"

"Don't know. Same guy who called thirty minutes ago."

Someone checking up on her? Already? Had Aunt Katherine made a complaint against her after all? She was only thirty minutes late.

"Hello?" She perched on the sagging edge of the only chair in the tiny living room.

"Hi. Lisa?"

"Yeah?"

"Oh. Glad you're home. This is Ethan Vale."

"Ethan? Oh, hi." What did he want?

At Uncle Fred's raised brows, she waved him away. He punched the TV's off button, then left the room, heading toward the kitchen for his usual bedtime snack of crackers and milk.

"Beth Anne asked me to call to make sure you got home all right. And she wants to know if you'd like a ride to the Bible Study at Jimmy's house. That came up after you left, I guess. We're starting tomorrow night."

"Who else will be there?"

"Not too sure. Cindy and Pam, probably. Me and Jimmy. We can arrange a ride for you, if you need one. Beth Anne said you might."

Another gathering so soon? And Lisa

wasn't too keen on Bible Study. It sounded dry. All that stuff about people dead thousands of years? What would their lives have to do with hers? Up until now, she'd depended on Beth Anne to show her the Scriptures she could apply to her life.

*What do you have to lose but ignorance?*

The small urging came gliding through her thoughts. She'd had more of the same lately, and she found it a bit spooky sometimes. But Beth Anne thought it perfectly natural in a believer.

"Okay." The sudden acceptance popped out of her mouth before she realized it. "I work later on Fridays. I need to get stuff ready for the evening shift. If someone can pick me up at the restaurant where I work, I'll come. Uncle Fred is usually out on weekends, so I don't have his car."

"Great. I'll make sure to be there on time."

*He* would? If Ethan Vale thought this was some kind of date, then he had a rude awakening. No dating for her now or in the future, and even if there were, she sure wouldn't choose a self-absorbed easy charmer like Ethan Vale. She was through with men. Totally, forever through with men. Romance didn't work in her life, she'd painfully discovered. Besides, all the good men were taken.

But…if Ethan wanted to put himself out to help her, why should she care? She'd let him. His personal interest would be short-lived, anyway, because as soon as he found out about her recent troubles, he'd run scared. Men did that.

Meanwhile, she could use the promise of her new associations to impress her parole officer.

"Suit yourself."

In the background, she suddenly heard the wail of a small child. "Daddy…"

"Uh-oh, gotta go. See you tomorrow night."

The phone line clicked. He'd hung up.

So Ethan was a parent, too. What was his story?

It didn't matter. She set the phone back on the scratched mahogany end table, wondering how Ethan expected to pick her up from her place of work when she hadn't told him where to come. And how had he known she'd need a ride? What had Beth Anne told him?

# Chapter Three

"C'mon, Stacy." Against a background of three-year-old Jordan making "vroom-vroom" engine sounds and five-year-old Tony squabbling with seven-year-old Bethany over a Game Boy, Ethan pleaded with his sister. He shifted the phone receiver and plugged his other ear. "Please? I took your kids and mine to the zoo last month, remember? For the whole day."

"Ethan," his sister said reasonably, "taking the kids one time doesn't equal all the extra hours I've given you this past year. You have to find someone besides me to help with the kids. Like Sharon's parents."

He mumbled a not-very-nice comment about his in-laws as he watched his children. Tim and Barbara Long were impossible to please, they had never approved of him, and he strongly suspected that given half a chance, they would sue for custody of his children.

He ignored Stacy's suggestion.

"You tell me to get a life, but how can I do that without help, Stace?"

He heard his sister's long-suffering sigh. "You can't expect me to handle all your childcare problems, Ethan. Can't you ask Sharon's parents for a change?"

"Uh…I don't want to do that. Look, I have two job interviews lined up this week, and Sharon's mom agreed to pick up Bethany and Tony after school today. That's enough, okay? Jordan will be all right at nursery school for a bit. But I can't ask the Longs to watch them tonight. I just can't. They ask too many questions."

"Uh-huh, and I had the kids over last weekend while you hung out at that Roger guy's house. What were you doing all that time anyway? You were over an hour late picking them up."

"Yeah, but that Roger guy is a top fiddle player and we had a hot session. We're sounding better than ever, sis. Still Western swing, but fresher."

His sister sighed into the phone again. "Your band sounding good doesn't guarantee a steady living, Ethan. Can't you see it? You're riding a slippery slope here. If Sharon were alive…"

"But she isn't, Stacy," he said with a quiet reserve, "and I can't live the rest of my life in an image that no longer fits."

"Okay, okay. Sorry." Stacy sounded mollified, but continued scolding in her gentle way. "But when are you going to get a real job again? You've been out of work for almost five months, Ethan. Is either of these two interviews likely to bring you into the fold?"

Into Stacy's idea of a family fold, Ethan realized. He struggled with the expression for a few moments.

"Uh…well, maybe." He wasn't completely out of money yet. And he'd return to the banking world as a last resort. He found banking—numbers, mortgages, interest rates and stock market going up and down— boring. Interacting with people, having fun playing his music as he'd done in college— that was much more satisfactory.

Sharon had never agreed, and he'd gone along with her idea of the family fold. He'd settled into a seventeen-year banking career that had pleased both her and her parents. Oh, yeah. He'd made the money....

For a long time, he and Sharon had lived a great up-and-coming young professional's existence. He admitted he'd enjoyed part of it. They jaunted and partied, bought a mid-sized house in a snazzy lake community, and traded cars every three years. He liked to cook and often played chef for a host of friends, devising elaborate menus from TV chefs. People loved his dinners.

Sharon felt passionate about her career in retail upper management and had been happy enough to postpone having children. He'd been the nag, wanting children sooner rather than later, but he'd let Sharon choose her time. Then bing, bing, bing, three babies in less than five years.

And a year after Jordan was born, his wife had suddenly died of an unsuspected heart aneurysm.

Two years ago...two long years...rough years.

He'd plunged himself into caring for the children, getting through his demanding days at the bank with the promise of their welcoming smiles. For a long time that was enough. It kept him from crying too much, that unmanly pastime that he did only in the deepest night when nobody could see except God and himself.

His music soothed him, and from it he took encouragement. If only Stacy knew that he was digging himself out of the doldrums, she wouldn't scold him so much.

The house was always in shambles, though. A series of housekeepers helped a little, and he wasn't so pressured to run the vacuum or take care of laundry, but it seemed impossible to keep them.

Then this last year he'd slowly wakened to a feeling of overwhelming loneliness. He wanted adult company—*needed* other adults in his life. He also needed to change his life, make it count in a different way. Those feelings came just about the time his bank was merged into a larger one. His position disappeared, and he wondered—what next? Another bank?

He'd thought about it long and hard, for months now. He wanted a business of his own creation, one that appealed to him. And it would be totally different from banking.

Slowly a plan emerged.

He wanted a restaurant; not too large, and

with a small lead staff. He wanted a corner stage for a live musical group to entertain customers. It was a leftover dream from his college days, he knew, and he wasn't sure if he could make it work. But he wanted to try, to give it all he had. It would provide a place he could indulge his love of playing, of performing. It might not make him wealthy, but it would give him peace.

He'd tossed his ideas around with Mike Faraday. Mike had pointed out that perhaps God was giving him an opportunity for the change in his life that he desired.

To have a new beginning. And he agreed.

As his severance pay diminished, he'd sold the lakeside house and moved into smaller digs. Without Sharon, the fancy house felt too big, anyway. His profit from the sale gave him a financial cushion, but not enough to finance his restaurant scheme. He had to have solid backing, and he couldn't go much longer without a steady income, either.

Maybe he was a dreamer. Sharon wouldn't have approved, and neither had her parents when he'd mentioned the idea. He hadn't a jot of restaurant experience, they pointed out, and his chances of failure were high. Plus, they argued, he had an obligation to support the children in a way that their daughter would have wanted.

Still, the dream only grew stronger.

"Daddy, Tony's gonna hit me," Bethany declared, her little chin thrust out as she glared at her brother. Her voice yanked Ethan back to the situation at hand.

"It's *mine*," Tony insisted. The boy squinted defiantly at his sister, his small hands balled into fists.

Ethan swooped Tony up by the waist just as he let a fist fly, missing Bethany by inches.

"Okay, Stacy…"

Without a word to Bethany, Ethan set the squirming Tony on his feet, yards away from his sister. Then he took the Game Boy out of her hands, leaving her to sputter, and put it high on a kitchen shelf in time out.

"I'll make a deal with you," he said into the phone. "I'll watch your two while you and that hubby of yours take a getaway weekend."

"Now you're talking," Stacy crowed. "Fitch will be thrilled. Next weekend?"

"Ahh…next weekend…" He hedged, his thoughts rapidly reviewing his options. One whole weekend shot, but then he'd have achieved payback. And often, the kids fought less with their cousins around.

He hemmed a moment, then let his sister pounce.

"Next weekend, buddy boy, or it's a no-go. Fitch and I need a break. Two days and two nights."

"Two nights?" Hiding his elation, he teased her with an exaggerated groan. He couldn't let his sister think she'd let him off too easy.

"Yep. Friday and Saturday. And *you* provide tonight's pizza."

"All right, you got it. I'll see you soon."

He'd drop his children at Stacy's house on his way to pick up Lisa Marley.

Lisa wiped the last empty table in her station at the restaurant where she worked. The dinner rush in full swing, she headed toward the kitchen with a tray of dirty dishes. Returning, she refilled coffee cups for the lingering diners at table twelve, handed menus to the newly seated table ten, then checked the time. Thirty minutes till Sally came in at seven. Thirty minutes until her long shift ended.

She'd been on her feet since before the restaurant opened at six that morning. But Sally had needed a favor, and Lisa was glad for the extra time. Besides, tomorrow being Saturday, she'd work only a half shift.

And then on Sunday she could see Cecily. For two whole hours, she'd be allowed to play with her daughter. To hold her, talk to her. The thought was the only thing keeping her going....

Afterwards, maybe she'd borrow Uncle Fred's truck again to drive out to the evening service at Blue River Valley Community Church. Beth Anne talked so lovingly of the members there, Lisa hoped...well, maybe some of them wouldn't freak out if they knew she'd served time. She wouldn't tell them, though, not if she could help it.

Fingering her pocketful of change, Lisa gauged it to be about five or six dollars. Enough to buy Cecily a book if she had the time and opportunity to run by a store. Her tips in bills amounted to forty-eight dollars. Pretty good for a no-alcohol-served family eating place. Saturdays were always good.

Night tips were better. She'd take nights quick as a blink, except Mrs. Braddock thought it better for her to work days until she'd proved herself. And a year under Mrs. Braddock's watchful eye wasn't forever, she reminded herself.

Waitressing didn't pay as well as her office manager position had, and wasn't the easiest job in the world. But no one questioned past references too closely, either. And Lisa was learning to be good at the work.

In all probability, she'd never become the cashier. Too many doubts from her manager. Nor would she gain another job as an accountant-slash-office manager. Most firms didn't put much trust in a convicted embezzler.

Returning from filling salt shakers, she spotted a new customer at the counter. Ethan Vale.

His dark hair appeared loosely brushed and needed a trim. He folded his hands, resting them on the countertop as he acknowledged her slight nod. His mouth curved upward. She noted his short, clean nails. A man who kept his nails neat always impressed her.

"You're early." Without conscious thought, she smoothed the apron over the food-spattered white blouse. Perhaps it had been a mistake to agree to let him pick her up at work. She didn't want people from New Beginnings coming in here, snooping. She didn't want anyone at work to know of her personal life, either.

Besides, she hadn't had a chance even to brush her hair since noon, much less check her makeup. She handed him a menu.

"Yeah, got lucky," he said, flashing a half smile that did more than merely hint at charm. It lit his face with warmth and made her want to see that grin full-blown.

"Hope you know that's the only luck you'll get today," she snapped. Too much charm made her jittery.

He chuckled, his light-brown eyes gleaming with humor. "Not that kind of luck. I'm not looking. Well, not right away, I'm not. What I mean is my sis offered to take my kids to an animated movie with hers. They'll stay the night."

At the mention of his children, Lisa let a twist of envy dissolve before saying, "That's nice. But I can't leave until my replacement comes in. Want something while you wait?"

"Like what?" He shrugged off his denim jacket as though to settle down.

"You aren't eating supper here, are you?"

Dismay was evident in her tone, and she could have kicked herself for making him aware of her turmoil.

He raised a brow. "Coffee will do."

A surge of customers kept her busy after that. Sally rushed in, later than she'd promised, and by the time Lisa changed clothes in the ladies' room, they were already late for the Bible Study.

Ethan waited for her out front.

"Sorry," she mumbled as they reached Ethan's car, aware she was falling into an old pattern of apologizing for something she couldn't control.

Uncle Fred had dropped her off at work that morning. She hated to depend on anyone else for anything. It threw her into a panic of defense about causing so much bother. Men hated a bothersome woman.

"Was it your fault?"

"Not really, no."

"Then you don't have to apologize. You couldn't leave before now or you'd have left your employer in a bind."

She slid a glance his way. Did he really believe that or was he only being nice? She took a deep breath and let it out. He was right about one thing. She would no longer apologize for something that wasn't her fault or that she couldn't control.

"How far to Jimmy's house?"

"Twenty minutes. Relax. It's no big deal if we're a little late."

"So you say. It'll be over soon after we get there."

"On a Friday night? No one's likely to rush home."

True enough. Lisa hadn't thought of that. "I have to be home by ten."

"Ten?"

"Yes. Ten."

"Why?"

"I just do."

"Do you have a late date?"

Outraged, Lisa shot a glare his way. He stopped for a red light and returned her stare, his lids at half mast. "Well? It doesn't matter to me, I only want to know, since we're cutting our Bible Study down to a scant hour, what's so important."

"It's not a late date, but even if it were, it wouldn't be any of your business," she practically growled at him. How dare this man question her? "It's just something I have to do. Be home by ten. Every night."

"That's—"

"Don't say it. If you can't get me home by ten, then maybe you'd better let me out at the next convenience store with a phone."

She had her hand on the door handle.

"Don't be ridiculous. I'm not going to do that."

"I'm not ridiculous, only realistic."

"Leaving you stranded is ridiculous. Come on, Lisa. I'm sorry I was nosy. Sheesh! Lighten up, okay?"

"Fine. Let's just forget it. What's the study to cover tonight?"

He remained quiet for a moment.

"Dunno, but it wouldn't hurt if we took a look at Corinthians. First, thirteen."

"Why? What's that?"

"Oh, you know. Love is patient, kind, not rude and so on…"

This wasn't shaping up to be a fun evening, Lisa decided. That's all she needed—someone else to lecture her.

"You pompous jerk. I—"

"Slow down, Lisa," he said. "I meant me. *I* need that teaching. I couldn't begin to judge whether you do or not. Only you would know your own state of mind. Now let's call a truce, please?"

She remained silent as he parked the car

in the lot, then led her to Jimmy's townhouse. Once they were inside, they headed to opposite sides of the living room. Lisa found a place to sit on the floor with a cushion, remaining quiet throughout the ongoing Bible Scriptures and discussion.

At nine-thirty, while Ethan and Jimmy were totally absorbed in their music, Lisa quietly begged a ride home with Pam. Ethan didn't even notice her leaving, she thought as she slipped out the door behind Pam. She'd left Cindy to tell Ethan he'd lost one passenger to gain another. Cindy didn't have to be home until whatever hour she wanted.

"I sure appreciate this," she told Pam. "This way Ethan can stay as long as he likes."

"No problem," said Pam. "My boys are older now, so I don't have to rush right home. I can drop you off easily."

Partying, even innocently, was a thing of the past for her, Lisa mused as she slid into Pam's brown compact. She had to take all her activities seriously from now on. She had little room in her life for an irresponsible charmer.

At eleven-twenty, Uncle Fred's phone rang. Uncle Fred didn't own an answering machine, and he wouldn't be home till the wee hours of the morning. It was unlikely the call was from anyone other than Ethan.

Lisa let the phone ring. Ethan could be as mad as a rain-slogged rooster, but it wouldn't make a whit of difference to her. He'd go find another woman to charm.

Yet she counted the rings. Ten, eleven, twelve.

"Quitter," she muttered after the last one died away.

## Chapter Four

Lisa had come into work at six in the morning. She pushed the previous evening from her mind. No use thinking about it—it hadn't caused her to lose any sleep. Today was today and she had to put on a smile and be dependable and friendly to keep her job.

She prided herself on her good memory and had no trouble remembering orders. She had eight or nine tables to care for, depending on how efficient Josie, the other waitress, was. Lisa didn't mind the hard work.

Toward ten in the morning she discovered Ethan at table five. What was he doing here? She hadn't seen him come in.

When she arrived at his booth, his eyes were lowered as he studied the menu. Beside him, a small face peeped up at her, barely above the tabletop. One of his children, she supposed. The little boy stared at Lisa with wide, bright eyes.

Her guard went up. She wouldn't be suckered into liking the child. She couldn't afford to give any more love away. It hurt too much when it wasn't returned.

She stood waiting, pad and pencil poised, then said politely, "Hi. How may I help you?"

"Stop being mad at me," Ethan said without raising his eyes.

Her breath caught. How could he possibly read her like that? Know that she'd been miffed? No hello or how are you?

"I'm not mad at you," she said, denying his claim without emotion. "I'm not anything with you."

"Then why did you run out on me last night?" He looked up directly into her eyes.

Disconcerted, she blinked.

His brown eyes glinted softly, but they still demanded an answer.

She looked away, then back. She struggled to keep her cool. To keep her emotions under control. "You were busy. I didn't see what difference it made who took me home."

One dark brow lifted. "I did. I was

worried about you. When I'm responsible for seeing someone home, then you bet it makes a difference."

"Well, I…" Flushing with guilt, she felt like squirming while her mind searched for a reason. A legitimate one. In the past no one had called her on her excuses.

"And you didn't answer the phone," he accused.

She couldn't lie. That was something the old Lisa would've done in a New York minute. But she couldn't stand here talking all morning either, or she'd be in trouble. Her boss was already frowning at her.

"No, I didn't." She stood straighter, giving him a narrow-eyed stare. The truth wasn't that hard to deliver, she assured herself. But she supposed she had been a bit rude. "I'm really sorry." The words came out with a squeak. "Is that better? Now, may I please take your order?"

"Good enough, I guess. I'll have coffee and a sweet roll." He glanced at the child. "Jordan will have chocolate milk. Won't you, sport?"

Jordan nodded, smiling at Lisa as he snuggled against his father. His thick hair lay against his head smoothly, except where it stuck up against his father's arm. Lisa couldn't help herself—her fingers itched to brush it back in place. Her heart melted and she smiled down at him.

"Okay, one chocolate milk coming up," she said. "Coffee and sweet roll."

She hurried to fill Ethan's order, and when she returned to their table with their items, she glanced down at the two of them. Another customer took the seat in booth three, so she headed immediately to take her order.

Focused on her work, Lisa paid Ethan no more direct attention. Ethan didn't talk to her again, but when he left, he waved cheerily and smiled a friendly goodbye. The little guy smiled at her, too. Waving back, she realized he was about the right age to play with Cecily.

But would Ethan still want to be friends after he found out about her past? She didn't think so.

She couldn't allow him to become that close. It wasn't worth the risk of having the friendship fail. Besides, Cecily came first. That was all that mattered.

Without realizing it, Lisa relaxed. Ethan could be a pretty good friend, she guessed, if someone was looking for that. But she'd better keep him an acquaintance. His friendship was not for her.

On Sunday, Lisa had Uncle Fred's truck. She wasn't causing Uncle Fred any trouble. He liked to sleep late on Sunday, and then putter around his yard.

Excited, she'd dressed with extra care, wearing a brown print skirt and creamy blouse. They were new. Uncle Fred had given them to her especially for today.

Today was the day she'd see Cecily.

She drove to church, nerves already making butterflies in her stomach. The parking lot was almost full, so she chose a spot on the street.

*I can do this. I can go in, listen to the sermon and like it…God's word, after all, so it's bound to be good. Beth Anne said people were friendly….*

Lisa got out of the truck and strolled to the entrance of the main church building. She nodded a hello to the greeter and went in to the service. Taking a seat in the last row, her hands wrapped around the carved edge of the pew and she told herself to relax. Next to her, a family of four were busy getting settled. They didn't speak.

It was a good thing she'd been at this church once before, she thought as she looked around. It wasn't completely strange. Her jumping nerves quieted as the service began.

She spotted Beth Anne sitting with her husband and Pastor Faraday on chairs behind the podium. Beth Anne was wearing a stylish multi-print dress. Lisa had never seen her in anything but casual clothes before, or with her brown hair so sleek and shiny. She thought her friend looked gorgeous.

It was a rather formal service, unlike the lively Thursday-night gathering. Pastor Faraday gave the Scripture devotion and opening prayer, leaving the main sermon to Pastor Hostetter, Beth Anne's husband.

The sermon seemed to creep along. It wasn't half over before Lisa surreptitiously glanced at her watch. Two more hours till she could see Cecily.

*I could listen better if this wasn't the day, Lord. Help me to concentrate....*

Glancing about her, Lisa spotted a woman she'd noticed Thursday night. Tall, with hair as pale as moonshine, she was sitting with an older woman who shared the same hair color. A relative, no doubt. What was her name? Lisa wondered. Her expression was grave. Somber. What was she thinking? Was she unhappy about something?

The service finally came to a close. Lisa shot to her feet; she wanted to shove through the crowd, to get in the truck and speed her way to Aunt Katherine's.

But it was too early. Her aunt wouldn't be home yet from her own church service. She'd want time to relax and change clothes. She wouldn't let Lisa in before the arranged time, anyway. Not before one o'clock.

Lisa decided to linger, knowing Beth Anne would eventually come down to talk to her. She let the crowd go around her while she waited. Then two girls, both about twelve, ran up to Beth Anne and started talking.

The girls would be there forever, Lisa mused, so she turned to join the exiting crowd, jostled between an elderly man and a couple of teens. Pastor Faraday waited at the doors, greeting and shaking hands with worshipers. She didn't want to be acknowledged like the other worshipers, so she slipped by unnoticed; she felt a little lost among the strange faces anyway.

Outside, she paused. The October sun lay

half-hidden behind a cloud. She shivered and pulled her jacket collar closer.

It was only a little past twelve. What could she do until the appointed time?

"Lisa."

She turned to see Beth Anne, her brown hair bouncing about her shoulders, racing toward her. "Hi, Lisa. I'm glad I caught you. I'm so glad you came today."

"I wanted to come." And in spite of the slow-moving sermon, Lisa realized she *was* glad. She'd just been restless and preoccupied. Besides, going to church was a promise she needed to keep, and it might as well be this church as any other. This was God's house, after all. She needed to make new friends, and here, she at least knew Beth Anne.

"Who is that?" she asked, watching the tall woman she'd noticed inside move away from Michael Faraday while her companion remained talking. The woman limped badly, and her long legs were hidden by dark slacks and sturdy shoes. She managed to make her way toward the parking lot slowly. When she turned to see where her companion was, Lisa could tell that she was in pain. "Isn't she a member of New Beginnings?"

"Sharp eye, Lisa. Yes, that's Samantha." Beth Anne spoke tentatively, showing her concern for the woman. "Thursday was the first time for her at New Beginnings, as well. She needs friends, I think."

"She is *so* beautiful," Lisa marveled. "I'd think she'd have loads of friends already. She looks familiar, but I can't think why. And why is she limping?"

"A bad accident. And the reason she seems familiar is that she's a famous model. When she was younger, she was on the covers of many a magazine, under the name Samantha Kim. And you can't see it from this distance, but one side of her face is badly scarred." Beth Anne lowered her voice. "She needs plastic surgery, but…well, she came home to recover."

"Oh… I'm very sorry." Someone else who wanted to hide from life, Lisa guessed.

"Well, I really have to go." She suddenly wanted to share her excitement with Beth Anne. "I'm going to see my little girl today. Can you believe it? I can play with her—" and hug and kiss her, cuddle her, see her smile, hear her laughter "—for two whole hours!"

Beth Anne placed her hand on Lisa's arm,

her green eyes warm with empathy. "Oh, Lisa. How purely wonderful. I'm sure you'll be blessed by this afternoon. I'll pray the visit goes well. Call me afterwards, won't you? And tell me all about the visit?"

"Oh, yes. Yes, I will." Lisa felt a sudden gratitude toward her friend. "Thank you, Beth Anne."

Gratified that her friend wanted to hear about her first visit with her daughter, Lisa felt lighter. As she left the church, her elation flamed high with hope. She'd shared her feelings with a friend, something she had not done for a long time.

She climbed into the old rusted truck and picked up the fuzzy pink bunny she'd bought that morning for Cecily. She'd stopped at a convenience store for gas, and there it was on the counter. She couldn't resist it.

An enormous pink polka-dot bow circled the bunny's neck. She hoped her daughter liked the stuffed animal.

She would only be about fifteen minutes early now, if she drove at snail speed, Lisa figured, nibbling at her lower lip as she started the truck.

A short while later, she parked the truck in

front of Aunt Katherine's shotgun-style house. She glanced up the hard concrete steps to the wooden porch. As a teenager, she'd spent some tough times in that house. But Cecily was only three. She wasn't yet old enough to wonder why Aunt Katherine was such a harsh disciplinarian. She wouldn't be there long enough to suffer under the same difficult conditions as Lisa had.

Not if Lisa could do something to prevent it.

She wondered if her aunt and uncle were home from church. The garage was in the back of the house off the alley, and she couldn't see if the car was there. Should she wait in the truck or risk Aunt Katherine's wrath by knocking on the door?

She'd wait.

*Oh, dear Lord, please help me now. Please let this visit go well. I want so much for Cecily to love me…. I want her back, God. I had no choice when I left her in Aunt Katherine's care. I'll be a good mother, I promise! Oh, yes…without trouble from Aunt Katherine, if You can swing that. But knowing Aunt Katherine, I doubt it. Anyway, I just want today to go okay, all right? Thanks.*

She felt calmer. She always did after

praying, something she'd learned to do at Beth Anne's urging.

Taking out her small notebook, she checked her to-do list for the week. It didn't consist of much. Work, work and more work. But squeezed on the line for Thursday evening were the words *New Beginnings.*

Funny…she thought of the meeting she'd attended. It wasn't something she would have gone to before her prison term. Prison term… She might as well say it and be done with it. Nothing was the way the way it had been before; nothing was left from her old life.

Well…that was good, wasn't it?

She kept a watch on the house. At promptly one o'clock, she headed up the walk. She suppressed a desire to chase up there and pound on the door, but the thought made her smile slightly.

Aunt Katherine answered the door with her usual sober expression.

"All right. I saw you sitting out in front waiting—smiling as you came up here. Well, you might smile now, my girl, but I'm warning you. You behave yourself."

"Thank you, Aunt Katherine." Lisa used a demure voice. There would be no shouting today. No ugly talk.

Right away, she heard a child's chattering from the kitchen. Her child. Her heart felt like a drum, picking up its beat.

"Cecily?" Her voice was tentative as she walked toward the kitchen. She paused in the doorway.

The little girl, distracted by Lisa's voice, gazed up at her. Too big for a high chair, Cecily was dwarfed in the regular kitchen chair she was sitting in. She'd been eating lunch. A bit of green bean stuck to her chin.

"We left her in her Sunday dress for your visit." Aunt Katherine spoke as though she'd made a great sacrifice. She believed in changing clothes the minute a person returned home from church. "This one time."

Cecily wore a pink Sunday dress, with tucks and lace and little puffed sleeves. She looked so darling, Lisa thought, as though she'd stepped out of a picture book. But Lisa understood Aunt Katherine's message. There would be no repeat of this one kind thing she'd done for Lisa.

"That's nice of you," she acknowledged. "Thank you."

"We're just about through," Uncle Mark said. He lifted Cecily down from her chair, then grabbed a napkin to wipe her chin.

"Hi, sweetheart." Lisa bent over, her voice wobbling as she swallowed hard. Don't rush her. She hasn't seen you in such a long time. You have to get acquainted with her all over again.

"Hi," Cecily said, looking up at her with curiosity.

Lisa went to her knees to be on the same level. "I've come to see you especially. Do—do you know wh-who I am?"

The little girl shook her head.

"I'm your m-mommy. You used to live with me, do you remember?"

Fascinated, Cecily shook her head again.

"Do you remember the duck song?" Lisa began singing softly, "This little duck, once I knew…"

A light dawned in Cecily's eyes. She chuckled as Lisa sang. "Big duck, fat duck, little ones, too…"

Cecily laughed with glee. Lisa smiled too, elation filling her, and kept on singing. When she got toward the end, Cecily sang "Quack, quack, quack" right along with her.

"Of course, you remember," Lisa said, laughing, the tears streaming down her face.

"Why are you crying?" Cecily asked. "Do you have a boo-boo?"

"No, sweetie, I'm just happy to see you," Lisa explained. Unable to help herself, she gently brushed the curls from Cecily's forehead. Her little girl talked so much better now than when she'd left. In complete sentences.

Then she rose and pulled a tissue from her pocket to wipe her eyes.

"Why don't you go into the front room now," suggested Aunt Katherine, not unkindly for a change.

"Yes, let's do that," Lisa agreed. Brightly, she hoped, for Cecily's sake.

She held out her hand to her daughter. "I have a little gift for you."

Cecily hesitated, then placed her small fingers in Lisa's. They felt so soft and tiny. Lisa could feel each little one.

When they reached the front room, Lisa sank down on the edge of the sofa, where she'd dropped her package when she came in. Cecily leaned against her knees, and the contact with her little body nearly sent Lisa into tears again. She held the bunny out for Cecily.

A squeal greeted the offering. "Bunny!"

Cecily inspected the stuffed animal while Lisa inspected her. Her curls were a soft ash brown, her skin rose-colored. She had Lisa's eyes, and delicate hands like Lisa's mother. *Had this glorious child come from her? She's a gem...a beautiful gem,* Lisa thought.

After a few moments, Lisa handed her the book she'd also brought. Cecily tore at the wrapping paper. "A book!"

Cecily cuddled close beside her on the sofa, hugging the bunny, while Lisa read to her.

By the time Lisa's visit was coming to an end, Cecily's eyes were drooping. Lisa didn't have the heart to keep the little girl awake any longer. She carried the child to bed, helped her out of her dress, then tenderly tucked a light blanket over her. Cecily's eyes closed. Finally, Lisa knelt on the floor to watch her sleep.

She sat that way for ten long minutes.

"Time to go." Aunt Katherine had been very generous. She hadn't interfered with the visit.

"I know." Lisa didn't move.

"Lisa…"

"Yes, I'm going."

She rose, gave Cecily one last gentle kiss, then marched out. "I'll be back Thursday afternoon."

Aunt Katherine's voice took on its usual caustic tone as she followed Lisa toward the front door. "Yes, I expect you will. But be on time, please. And you can't spoil the child by bringing her presents each time you come. That'll have to stop."

Lisa stopped walking. She slowly turned to stare at Aunt Katherine. The woman would never cease trying to run Lisa's life. And she wanted permanent custody of Cecily?

Aunt Katherine had said nothing further about the custody issue. Maybe she'd dropped the idea.

Lisa clamped her mouth on a sharp retort. If she wasn't careful, her aunt's vindictive attitude could be catching. But now was not the time to challenge her.

"I'll stop after a time, Aunt Katherine. You are quite right, Cecily would come to expect them. I won't spoil her."

The older woman stared at Lisa with suspicion. She didn't seem mollified by Lisa's quiet capitulation. It only made her leery.

*Keep calm...give her a reasonable answer....*

Lisa cleared her throat and continued. "But just now, I want to give my daughter everything I can. I've been apart from her for eighteen months. I've missed eighteen months of her life. Can't you understand, Aunt Katherine? I can afford only little gifts now. I can't give her a home, or food, or clothing or…or…the things you've given her for those eighteen months. You needn't be jealous."

"I…jealous?" Aunt Katherine's mouth set in hard lines, and her voice became icy. "You mistake me, my girl. I am not jealous. What have I to be jealous about? But I warn you, Lisa. Don't give Cecily any more presents. It will be hard on the child when you stop. And I'll throw them out if you do."

Throw them out? Aunt Katherine would do it, too. She could be that mean, never giving a thought to how it might affect Cecily.

Lisa had to be careful not to give her aunt further reason to fight her return.

"All right, Aunt Katherine." Lisa kept her tone even. She'd made a mistake in implying jealousy. Her aunt didn't admit to such an emotion in herself. "I'll…see you Thursday."

Giving in to Aunt Katherine's demands galled Lisa. Just as in the old days, it would be hard to keep her anger down. But she must behave with the utmost care now. She didn't dare stir her aunt to greater ire.

Yet Aunt Katherine's threat lingered.

## Chapter Five

Lisa curled herself into a ball that night, buried her face against a pillow and cried herself to sleep. She had to get Cecily back. She missed her so....

And if left to Aunt Katherine's rules, Cecily was likely to turn into a royal little robot...or rebel.

No...no, she couldn't let her daughter turn out the way she had.

The smothered sobs came as hard as they had when she'd first been sent to prison. She hadn't wanted to leave her little girl, or give over custody to Aunt Katherine. But the alternative was to place Cecily into the foster care system, and what choice was that? There wasn't anyone else who could care for little Cecily except Aunt Katherine. And

Lisa hadn't wanted her child to see her mother in prison, either.

She cried now because she was free to see her daughter twice a week. She cried because she wanted to keep her each and every day.

She cried because the whole thing was so insanely unfair. In the past, Aunt Katherine had had reason to mistrust her.

But not anymore…

Lisa stuffed her mouth against the pillow so Uncle Fred wouldn't hear her. No need to make him miserable just because she was. And Thursday would come soon enough, Lord willing. She'd see her darling again.

*Oh, Lord, it isn't fair to separate me from my child.*

Fair or not, that was the way it was. Lisa had to prove herself responsible to Aunt Katherine. But Cecily couldn't live with Lisa until Lisa could provide a home for her. And providing a home was months down the road.

At least she had hope, and that sustained her. *Cast all your anxiety on Him because He cares for you….*

Where had she heard those words? From Michael Faraday at New Beginnings? She must have. She clung to them now, hoping there was truth in them.

As she fell asleep on a last quavering breath, she vowed she'd cried her last tear. No more. *Do You hear that Lord? Not one more tear! I'm through with feeling sorry for myself. I'm not going to cry anymore because I was dumb enough to fall for the flattery of that crazy stinking rat Rudy, and dumb enough to get caught up in his plans.*

Sighing, she indulged in her favorite fantasy. A fantasy of revenge, total and sweeping.

Okay, so she'd fallen for a well-laid embezzlement scheme. That was what made her feel so low now. Even though she'd known what he was doing was wrong, and felt as guilty as green slime, she'd still allowed that too-good-looking Rudy to pull the fast shuffle. She'd believed his lies about his "sick wife", too. Believed the woman was terminally ill, and that was the reason Rudy had put Lisa's name on all the telltale documents. She'd since learned his wife was hale and hardy, and probably laughing at Lisa all along.

She hated and despised Rudy for that most of all. She shuddered at the way she'd melted at the thought of how harsh Rudy's life was, and how difficult.

Rudy had used her. Simple and sweet. Used her compassion and love for him. But when all was said and done, he'd given her sweet Cecily. Thank goodness, all the while denying his paternity, but that was the only thing she could thank him for. He'd denied paternity, but Cecily was better off without him.

Well, that was the good thing, wasn't it? The really good thing? He didn't want any part of Cecily.

Never again would she trust any man. Never again would a man make her cry.

She settled herself more cozily under her blanket in the daybed in Uncle Fred's spare room and dreamed of a suitable punishment for the snake. Mere imprisonment was too good for Rudy, but she'd delight in that. Long periods of isolation for the skunk. Days without food. And of course her favorite image: dipping him in tar and then rolling him in tons of feathers. All in public, so that people could sneer and point. They'd know…

Thoughts of revenge had kept her sane those first days in prison, when she'd suffered in silence. Days and weeks and long months without her little girl.

Lisa woke in the morning feeling better, but with the idea of finding Rudy and making him pay still nagging her. This was the first time she'd thought of actually going after him. It was obscene that he'd gotten away with all that money. She figured the slimeball was on a beach somewhere where it was always warm, living life high on the hog, martini in hand. She'd stake her life on it.

"What is it, Lisa girl?" Uncle Fred asked as he drove her to work. 'You been smiling to yourself half the morning. Just last night, you was a bit tearful, too. Didn't you have a good visit with little Cecily? I maybe could borrow her from your Aunt Katherine come Sunday, and we could cook a little supper together. Nothing to object to in that, is there?"

"Oh, thanks, Uncle Fred." She hugged his arm. "You are a dear person. But Aunt Katherine isn't going to let go of Cecily that easily. Anyway, I was thinking of Rudy."

"You ain't still wishing on him, now, are you?"

"Oh, mercy, no. The thought of getting mixed up with Rudy again makes me sick to my stomach. No, I was thinking of how to catch up to the rat, that's all. How to trace

him down. If we could only find him, maybe
he'd have to serve time himself. If he serves
time, then maybe…I don't know, maybe I
could ease some of my guilt. But his
wife…well, there isn't anything we can do
about her."

As Uncle Fred dropped her off at the restaurant, Lisa realized once again that she
didn't know where Rudy was. She'd have
time to go to the library on Friday to use the
computers there to access the Internet. Rudy
could try to hide, but she knew his habits,
and she knew how to search. She'd start as
soon as she could.

On Thursday night, after a long and busy
day at work, Lisa drove to New Beginnings
once more. A little early, she sat in the
parking lot and watched the other arrivals.
She wasn't nearly as nervous as last week,
nor as tired. Still, she begged the Lord to be
with her.

*I've got to do better, Lord. I want to help
here at this church. Please help me.*

Lisa climbed out of the truck and walked
into the building. Recognizing several faces,
she nodded shyly, said hello to Michael
Faraday, and took a seat toward the rear. She

looked around for Beth Anne. Was her friend here tonight? Beth Anne had told her she couldn't come to every meeting.

Michael came forward, then spotting her, made a detour to where she sat.

"Glad to see you here, Lisa." He leaned against a chair in the row in front of her. She thought him attractive, with his dark looks, but too somber. Why was that? "I'd like to talk with you about something. Beth Anne says you have office experience and might be willing to help us out."

"Well, yes…" Lisa felt a bit leery. Was he going to say something about her former position?

"We have a seminar coming up and we could use your help."

"Me? What with?"

"Beth Anne tells me you have great organizational skills. That's just what we need. This seminar will attract lots of people, I'm thinking, and we need someone to keep track of registration. It isn't hard. We just need someone to take care of it. You don't have to call anyone or sell anything. How about it?"

She didn't know what to say. Sure, she could do that, but…Beth Anne had recommended her?

Had Michael heard about why she was in prison?

"Would I be working with someone?"

"Oh, sure. We'll find someone for you to team with."

"Well, I guess I could." She couldn't turn down Dr. Faraday and was flattered he'd asked her. "But I don't know...that is, I know only a few people here, and I've been here such a short time. Besides, I don't have anyplace to work. That is, I don't have a place of my own yet. I intend to, as soon as I have enough money, but...."

She blushed. Why had she blurted that out? She waited for Michael's response.

He paused for only a second. He must know...

But he said only, "You don't need a place of your own, Lisa, if that's all you're worried about. You can work here. On your own time."

"By myself?" With money in those registrations? "That is, don't you want, um... don't you want someone to work with me? Oversee everything?"

"Well, you might find it more enjoyable if you do that, and Beth Anne will be around some of the time, but I...who could we get to work with you? I guess Cassie, or Pam… or even Ethan?"

He was serious. He actually wanted her to do this for the group.

"What's the seminar about? I mean, I remember you talked about it last week."

"It covers the goals of New Beginnings. What we try to do here. How to start again with life. Changing directions, changing attitudes and reaching out for new goals. What God wants us to do with our lives. Putting on the new mind of Christ."

Putting on a new mind?

That stilled her. Beth Anne had been teaching that concept in the prison class, she reminded herself. For the women there.

Lisa thought of actually putting on a new mind. Behaving differently—leading a new kind of life. She'd struggled with that repeatedly since she'd left prison, but now she thought she could use that teaching again.

Only no one had told her it was so *hard*.

Working for the seminar would be a good thing. It would give her something to think about besides getting her daughter back. And plotting revenge against Rudy.

She wouldn't think of revenge. She'd concentrate on Cecily. And this seminar.

"All right, I'll do it. But my hours might be a little odd. I can't say exactly when I'll be able to put in the time. But I hope your seminar is a huge success."

"Great! I'll contact you when we need you. Actually, we have a few registrations already. Can you get them before you leave tonight? We can set up a bank account to handle the money tomorrow. Or as soon as you're free. Now excuse me, please. It's time we started tonight's meeting."

He headed back to the front of the group. She glanced about her, feeling stunned to be asked to help. And he wanted her to take charge, take home the registrations to work on. Beth Anne had suggested her, of course. Should Lisa be grateful or irritated? Never mind, this was work she was familiar with and she could do it without half trying.

She *was* good at organization—organizing an office anyway. Perhaps Beth Anne had suggested Lisa to draw her more solidly into New Beginnings.

Or to give her the gift of trust?

It dawned on her then; someone trusted her once again. A slow feeling seeped like honey along her veins. Someone trusted her to take care of registration and handle the fees involved. Trust was a gift. Deep-seated, no-holds-barred, gut-level trust.

She felt humbled and on the verge of tears. She sniffed, then raised her head, chin thrust forward. She'd be faithful to Beth Anne's trust, and thankful for it.

Where was Ethan Vale? She had to tell him…

Why? And tell him what? Just because he'd come to the restaurant where she worked to make sure she was okay?

That showed real concern. It was something a friend would do. But why did he care?

Don't you mean, why do I care? Her thoughts raced with the knowledge that she did care. His concern meant more than she'd bargained for.

Then she spotted him, jumping up with his guitar to open their meeting, his good looks and charm shining for all to see. He smiled her way, and she caught herself responding. Next to her, she heard a soft sigh, and she turned to see who it was.

Cassie…a gentle plump woman who had the dreamy eyes of a teenage groupie.

Well, Lisa wouldn't be one of Ethan's groupies…or followers. She'd already made that mistake, hadn't she?

Michael preached on thankfulness that night. Lisa's heart felt near to bursting. She *was* thankful….

Ethan sat on a navy-blue, straight-backed chair in a private office with sand-colored walls, waiting for the bank officer to speak. He hadn't come for a job. Ethan had applied for a business loan, and already he knew the answer was a no. He should have known—he would have turned down such an application, too.

The guy's name was Richard Dirking, someone Ethan knew well. He knew a great many people from the banking world.

"I'm sorry, Ethan, but the bank just doesn't want to make a loan of that size based on such a sketchy outline. You don't have a location, or a building plan for your restaurant, nothing. You just don't have enough solid information here. What are you thinking, anyway? You just have a few ideas."

"That's fine, Richard. I was merely testing the waters, I guess."

"Well, come back when you have something more concrete. Perhaps then we could help you. Meanwhile, how about lunch one day next week?"

Ethan rose and shook Richard's hand.

"Sure, Richard. Lunch next week would be great."

He left the bank and got into his three-year-old car. He sat a moment and thought of just where he wanted to land, what part of the city. Where did he want his restaurant to be located? Out in the suburbs? Or smack in the middle of the city? Oddly, it made him itch to start planning. He'd known his stop at the bank was premature, but his thoughts were swirling with the need to get something lined up.

All of a sudden, he knew he was going ahead with his dream. Despite all the reasons he shouldn't, he was going to make it happen. Elation reached down to his toes and he felt like calling Lisa Marley and celebrating. She would be the one to tell. She could use a little cheering up herself, and she'd think him just crazy enough for pursuing his scheme.

Besides, she was a cute little package, with a neat, compact body. But it was her eyes that made him pause. He'd caught something soulful there, some deep longing. And that haunted gaze made him want to find out why it was there.

He supposed grief had made him more sensitive. And he recognized a grieving Lisa—one she kept hidden.

A quick glance at his watch told him he had to pick up Jordan at the preschool. Then he needed to be home in time for Tony to arrive from kindergarten.

Ethan sped along the streets in amazement. All the months he'd been out of a job and he was suddenly galvanized to action. Why now?

The timing was right…for him anyway. For months he'd been asking the Lord for a sign as to how to go on and what to do. There hadn't been a clear answer, only a muddled one, yet he felt the Lord with him just the same. This was the right answer for him.

He wanted to see Lisa.

Why not treat the boys to lunch? Never mind that the restaurant was a bit out of his way. His sons would enjoy a change from peanut butter and jelly sandwiches at home.

Forty minutes later, he and the two boys stood waiting at the restaurant's reception desk. Two other parties were there as well.

"I'm sorry, but—" he spotted Lisa carrying a heavy tray behind the counter "—I'll wait for a booth to be free in Lisa Marley's station if you don't mind."

"Not at all." Showing only a hint of surprise, the dark-haired hostess agreed to his request. "But it will be a few minutes until one is free."

"No problem." He moved away from the front of the line.

"Dad, I'm hungry. Why can't we eat?" Tony tugged at Ethan's hand.

Ethan leaned down to whisper in Tony's ear. "We will, I promise you. And this place has the best burgers in town."

"French fries," Jordan said. He grabbed Ethan's hands to swing.

"Yeah, and French fries, too." He might as well face it—the boys would stuff their faces and tell Bethany. His daughter would demand equal time, and he'd have to take her out. Except for fast foods, eating out at restaurants had become a treat in the past year or so.

The hostess beckoned, and the three followed her to a booth toward the back of the restaurant. A few moments later, Lisa came over.

"Well, hello…" She gazed past Ethan to the boys, and her mouth softened into a smile. They smiled in return.

"Hi, Lisa," Ethan greeted her. "You're very busy, I see."

"Yes, it's lunch time." She stated the obvious with a straight face. "People usually become hungry around now. What may I get for you?"

"I want a hamburger…and French fries." Tony made his wishes known.

"This is Tony," Ethan said, indicating his older son. "He's a little impatient."

"Me, too," Jordan added, referring to the burger.

"Uh, bring one order, if you don't mind. These guys have eyes bigger than their stomachs."

"There's a children's menu on the back," she suggested. "It serves smaller appetites."

"Oh, yeah. A lapse of memory, I suppose." He turned the menu over. He hadn't really forgotten, but it was fun to keep her with him a little longer. "Okay, two servings of burgers and fries from the children's menu. Milk, too. And a chicken sandwich for me, and coffee, please."

"That's two children's plates of burgers and fries, milk and one chicken sandwich with coffee. Will that be all?"

"For now. Do you get a break anytime soon?"

She glanced back at the counter. "Not for another hour or two. Why?"

"I just thought you could sit with us a

while. I've been thinking about something, and I—I could use some adult advice."

He knew he was playing the sympathy card. He put his need in his gaze, hoping her compassion would extend to him. Why did he find her opinion so important?

She was the first woman since Sharon…

That was it. He hadn't been attracted to a woman since his wife died.

Why did he find Lisa so attractive? Because she was playing hard to get? He didn't think so.

She seemed to like the boys, who were fiddling with the salt and pepper shakers.

"I'd appreciate it if you could."

She glanced back at Ethan and studied him a moment before saying, "I have to put in your order now." She moved off abruptly, and he sighed.

Perhaps he was pushing. He seldom knew when he pushed too far. His sister often told him he did, and Sharon had said his charm wouldn't always get him what he asked for. But for the moment, that was all he had going for him.

Charm, he'd noticed, did get him most places. But Lisa was a challenge.

## Chapter Six

On Thursday evening, Ethan had nowhere to leave his kids and no one to stay with them, either, so he took them along to New Beginnings. What could it hurt? He had gone crazy all day; he'd been home all week without an adult for company. He loved his kids, but he'd go bonkers if he didn't find someone with whom to carry on an intelligent conversation.

Tonight, his sitter had cancelled at the last minute and he couldn't get anyone else on such short notice. He'd hurriedly stuffed drawing paper and crayons, a glue stick, pencils and scissors into a plastic bag and the kids into their coats and the car. They could draw while he played his guitar.

He sincerely hoped that would be the case.

He'd been playing his guitar a lot lately, moody, forlorn stuff. Where the dark mood came from, he had little idea, but it relieved some of his frustration. Oddly, he didn't think of Sharon as much. He supposed he was always focused on immediate demands, and the pressure to meet them sometimes laid him low.

"Come along, short stuffs," he said cheerily as he turned into the church lot and parked his car. "We're late, but we are here." He glanced at the three children, bundled to their eyes in coats and hats.

"Now, this meeting is for grown-ups, see? I want you to behave while Daddy is playing guitar." He'd lifted Jordan out of his car seat and was still holding him. The little boy smelled of peanut butter, and Ethan wondered briefly if he'd missed a spot. He distinctly recalled washing Jordan's face.

Too late now, he mused, setting his son down. Anyway, no one would care.

Then he reached for his guitar case. "There aren't any other kids here, so you'll have to entertain yourselves. Please, be quiet when someone's talking. There will be treats to eat afterwards if you're good."

"Will we have a table to draw on?" asked

ever-practical Bethany. "A table is the best, but we can use the floor if we have to."

"I can draw a Thanksgiving turkey with my hand," said Tony. "My teacher showed us." Then he made a face. "I like drawing roads and mountains for my cars, but I'll draw a turkey, if you want me to."

"I don't know about a table." Ethan led them into the church. "We'll see."

"Can we have some juice?" Tony asked. The boy was nearly running, and Ethan realized his usual pace was too fast for the children.

The members of New Beginnings would hear them coming, too, if they weren't quieter.

"I guess you can." Ethan stopped and said in a lower tone, "Here, Jordan." He put his case down on the floor and swung the child up to his shoulders.

Jordan giggled loudly.

Ethan let a low groan escape. "Shh. Use your indoor voices."

He drew a deep breath. He hoped it was all right that he'd brought his kids. No one else did.

It had to be okay. He'd had no choice. He wasn't going to stay home just because he didn't have a sitter.

So far, New Beginnings didn't provide child care, but he felt it only a matter of time until it did. Surely others had the same problems as he did.

"Why aren't there any kids, Daddy?" Tony asked.

"Well, most people let their kids stay home with a sitter so they can go to bed on time."

"I'm glad we don't have a sitter," Bethany said.

"Why is that?"

"'Cause then we get to go with you. That's more funner."

"Well, it's not a regular thing, so don't expect to do this in the future." He spoke firmly, but had little hope of making an impression. His kids would fuss at not going to the next meeting.

It was a busy evening at New Beginnings. People were still talking, and he hurried to get his kids settled. He shuffled them toward the wall, quickly taking off their coats. When he spotted a table in the back corner, he led his children there. After getting them seated and taking out the coloring things, he kissed each one on the cheek. "Now, be good for me, please, while Daddy plays his guitar."

"Can we have juice now?" Tony whispered.

"Yeah, juice..." echoed Jordan.

"Okay, I'll see what I can do. You sit here, okay? And don't bother anyone either. I'll be right back."

The meeting was about to start. Feeling a bit desperate, Ethan went to the kitchen, where a couple of the women were just leaving.

"Hi, Pam." He snatched the first woman he met. Pam was a pal, she'd understand. He'd known Pam, a small blond woman in her forties, for years, ever since she and her husband, a fireman, had opened accounts at the bank where he used to work. Pam had been widowed recently when her husband had died in an accident. "I had to bring my youngsters tonight. No sitter."

"Yes, I see you did." She glanced beyond him, out the kitchen door. "What do you plan to do with them?"

"They'll be fine if I can get them some juice. Any chance of that?"

"I think we can find you something. Here, these are smaller cups." She brought out three plastic cups from the cupboard. "Better for little hands, I think. Why don't you go on back to the kids and I'll bring the juice."

"Thanks bunches, Pam."

Ethan sighed with relief. The juice was a godsend. When he returned to the children, he told them their drinks were coming. In a low voice, he cautioned each child to be careful about spilling, then left them to take his place in the front of the gathering crowd.

Over thirty people tonight. Awesome.

He started tuning his guitar, but kept his glance at the far table. Bethany was bent over her paper while Tony and Jordan watched the crowd over the backs of their chairs. It sure beat drawing turkeys, he guessed.

There was a lull in the conversations, and Michael stepped forward. "Let's open with a prayer."

As Michael began the prayer, Ethan could hear the soft whispering of his children drifting out over the room. "No!" Jordan's sharp little voice was instantly recognizable.

Oh, boy! Ethan frowned at them, but they weren't looking at him. How could he discipline them when they paid him no mind?

Michael ignored them, thank the Lord. Sign of a good man, Ethan thought.

The whisperings and restlessness became louder. Giving up, he laid his guitar down and half rose to go and see what the matter was—and enforce silence on his children.

Then from the corner of his eye, he saw a woman creep toward them, slender and shapely in her blue jeans.

Lisa.

She held a finger to her lips and smiled the brightest smile he'd ever seen her give. It glowed. She picked up Jordan and cuddled him, her mouth slightly puckered as if she wanted to kiss him. She sat down in Jordan's chair.

The wonder of it was that Jordan let her hold him.

Tony turned to her and said something, but his voice was so low Ethan couldn't hear him. Only Bethany gazed at Lisa with open curiosity.

Michael said "Amen," and the evening started.

Amen...

Lisa hadn't planned to sit with Ethan's children until she found herself getting up and going to them. She held little Jordan, letting him wiggle and draw around her hand the way Tony showed him until the end of the evening's teaching.

As soon as the meeting was finished, Ethan hot-footed it over to them, and Lisa reluctantly offered him her chair. Jordan reached for his daddy, and she started to rise, letting the little boy go. Automatically, Ethan's hands wrapped around Jordan's little body, and Lisa felt the emptiness.

She let her own hands fall to her sides.

"Thanks, Lisa. Thanks a lot. My regular sitter had an emergency, and my sister couldn't watch them tonight, and I couldn't get another sitter…so I thought I'd just bring them. I didn't want to miss a meeting."

He spoke like the harried parent he was.

"That's okay, Ethan," she said, smiling at the children. "We had a good time, didn't we, Jordan?"

The little guy nodded.

"That's great. You guys want something to snack on now? We can't stay too long, y'know."

"Yay! Snacks!" Tony made his wishes known.

"Well, let's go. There's pretzels, I hope. And I saw cookies when I got the juice."

The table held several platters of cookies.

"Try some of these chocolate chip ones," Pam said, and pushed the plate of big round cookies with dark blobs in the middle toward the children. "I made them, and my kids love 'em."

The kids each took one, then glanced at Ethan.

"Okay, two," he said. "It's a special occasion. You can have two, but that's all. With any luck, this is the only time I'll bring you, unless it's a family thing."

"Okay," Tony said. "But I don't want to come anyway. It's boring."

"Well, that's just fine with me. It's not boring for me. Now eat up. It's late for you and Jordan."

"Not for me, Dad. I'm not grumpy." Bethany spoke with the righteousness of the firstborn.

Lisa chuckled, and Ethan threw her a "be quiet" look. But it was the first time he'd heard her laugh, and the deep-throated sound delighted him.

He spoke to the children. "Well, I've got to get you right into bed and to sleep the minute we get home. There's school tomorrow."

Lisa glanced at the clock over the kitchen door. It wasn't that late, but she, like the children, had to keep to a schedule. There was time to visit for a few more minutes, then she should take care of business.

"I have to pick up the registrations for the seminar," she said to Pam. "Where would I find them?"

"In the office, I'm sure."

"Has Pastor Faraday said…has he asked if you would work with me? I can organize and keep the registration straight, but I'd just as soon someone else handled the money. It should be put in a bank account until it's needed." Lisa held her breath. "Can you do that?"

"Hmm…not tomorrow. I'm up to my neck in togetherness with my husband's mother, then my mom. I just don't think I'll have time." Pam rearranged the cookies to fill in the empty spaces. "I'm really sorry, Lisa. Can it wait until the next day?"

"I'd rather not," Lisa said pensively. She wouldn't admit to the anxiety that crawled up her spine at the thought of taking care of that money.

"I can take care of opening an account, Lisa." Ethan was standing nearby, watching his children play. "I have the time."

"Will you?" She felt an easing in her spirit. "That's great."

"Sure. I used to be in the banking world. I know about this stuff."

He'd been in the banking world? Lisa's heart sank. She felt the blood drain from her face.

Each profession had its own inner circle. What would he know of her? Would he have heard of the scandal after she was sent to jail for embezzling? Perhaps. Would he turn his back on her now?

"My job was eliminated out when Blue River Valley sold to Bowers. I'm unemployed at the moment, but only because I want to be."

Her heart began to recover. He must have been quite high up in the bank's management. She wanted to place a hand over her pounding heart, but kept both of them at her side. Blue River Valley... That wasn't the bank where she'd been in trouble. Maybe he hadn't heard about her after all.

"I'll—I'll just get the registrations from the office," she said, blinking hard. "We can open them and you can take charge of the money—or checks—right now. I'll be right back with them."

She hurried toward Michael. He was standing with a couple of men, talking. The tall blond man looked at her with interest when she approached.

"I am sorry to interrupt, Pastor," she said, "but if you want me to work on the registrations, I'd better get them now. Ethan said he'd take care of the money and open a bank account to hold the fees. Um, shall I get someone else to be a secondary signature?"

"Oh, yes, Lisa. That's great to draw on Ethan's expertise. Here, we need to see…" He looked around the chatting crowd. "Let's see who's available. Pamela? Or Cassie?" Michael made a quick decision. "Yes, I think Cassie's an excellent choice. Why don't you come along and I'll introduce you."

Michael excused himself from his companions and led Lisa over to a plump woman, whose brown hair hung straight without styling. Lisa remembered her from before. Cassie smiled at their approach, and Lisa felt immediately comfortable with this woman.

Once introductions were made, someone called Michael's name and he left.

"So you want help with registrations?" Cassie asked. "Right now?"

"Well, I thought so… I just don't want to handle the money." Lisa brushed her hair back, hoping she wasn't too obvious. "Just the registrations, if that's all right. Ethan said he'd be glad to open the account, but we need a secondary signature?"

Cassie peeked around Lisa at Ethan, her eyes bright.

"Okay, I'll take them. Ethan and I can open the account tomorrow after school. I teach fifth grade, and I can't go till then. If that's all right with you?"

"Oh, yes. That's great." Lisa was so relieved she thought it must show in her face. "We can get started on the registrations then, and let people know we've received them."

"I gotta get these rugrats home to bed." Ethan came up to them, Jordan hanging from one arm and Tony holding the other. Bethany trailed behind them. "They're up way past their bedtime."

"It's been fun to see you guys," Cassie said shyly. "I have to get home, too. For school tomorrow. Ethan, I'll call you about setting up a time at the bank, okay?"

"Sure. Anytime."

They walked outside together, the children hopping about. Cassie hesitantly waved and got into her car.

"That worked out well," Lisa remarked.

Ethan stood by his car, fingering his keys, watching the kids run up and down the parking lot. He acted as though he didn't want Lisa to go just yet.

"Yeah, it did. Say, Lisa…can you have lunch with me tomorrow?" He blurted it out. "What time do you get off work?"

He was asking for a date?

It had been a long while since she'd been on a real date. She wasn't sure it would work.

"I don't know…I've been putting in long hours. I don't think dating would be such a good idea, Ethan."

"I only invited you to lunch." He sounded quite irritated. "It's not a major issue, Lisa. I only meant…"

He let his breath go, long and hard, then spoke softly. "I'd like a little bit of adult company. You know, a meal together where we both sit down? And nothing is spilled?"

She was tempted. "I'll think about it."

"Okay." He made a face. She wasn't giving in easily. "I'll call you tomorrow morning."

"Kids?" Ethan called.

The kids were huddled around a small dog. The poor thing was shivering as it ducked behind the wheel of Lisa's truck.

"What have you got, kids?" Lisa asked as she walked over.

Tan and short-haired, the dog appeared to be a mutt. Whenever the children held out a hand to it, it whined, backing farther behind the wheel. Yet anyone could see that it wanted attention.

"It's hurt," Bethany said, worried. "See, Daddy? He's been bleeding from that cut. Can't we get him and see what's the matter?"

"No, don't touch it, Bethany. Strange dogs sometimes bite." Ethan spoke with firmness. "Besides, he could be sick. We don't know what might be wrong, besides the scrapes."

"Whose dog is it?" Tony said. "Maybe we can find his home."

"I don't think she has a home," Lisa said. "She's not wearing a collar."

Was the dog female? Ethan's first inclination was to bend over and look at the dog more closely, but he was caught up in Lisa's expression and couldn't turn away. A haunting sadness shadowed her eyes, and for the first time Ethan wondered where Lisa lived. And with whom.

"We have to fix it, Daddy," Bethany insisted, nearly in tears. "It's hurt."

With all the responsibility he had right

now, Ethan really didn't need a dog to take care of. But he supposed he could drive it to the animal shelter. The people there would find a home for it—her. Whatever. He was about to say so, when Lisa spoke.

"I'll take her." She sat on her haunches and held a hand out to the dog. "C'mon, pooch. It's all right, I won't hurt you."

"He's all yucky," Tony said, also reaching out for the dog. "And he stinks."

"No, don't, Tony." His father was cautious. "Lisa…"

Paying him no mind, she spoke soothingly to the dog, all the while holding out her hand. In it, she had a cookie.

"You're okay, yes, you are," she said in a crooning kind of way. "You've just gotten yourself into a scrap, I think."

The dog crept out, then quick as a snap, grabbed the cookie and wolfed it down.

"I'll take you home with me and fix those wounds for you," Lisa said, putting her arms around the shivering creature. The dog struggled a bit, then quieted. "Uncle Fred won't mind." Her tone softened. "In fact, I think Uncle Fred will love you."

So, she lived with her uncle? It was the first Ethan had heard her mention him. He studied her as she slowly put her hand on the dog's head. Suddenly he realized he knew very little about Lisa.

And he wanted to know more…much more.

# Chapter Seven

Lisa parked the truck, then as gently as she could, carried the dog into the house. The mutt whimpered pitifully.

The dog smelled awful, filling the air with the stench of garbage and making Lisa's nose twitch. Tony was right—she'd have to give the mutt a bath first thing.

Uncle Fred, his glasses slipping down his nose, was just about asleep in his chair. "Whatcha got there, Lisa?"

"It's a mutt, Uncle Fred. A female. She was hanging out in the parking lot of the church." Lisa couldn't bear the thought of leaving the dog to roam the streets all night. "She was frightened and lost, I think. I hope you don't mind my bringing her home. She's been in a fight of some kind, and she's hurt. And hungry, if I'm not mistaken."

Uncle Fred pushed his glasses into place and struggled to rise. "A stray, huh? I'll find something for her to eat while you tend to her wounds."

"You don't mind, do you? That I brought her home?"

Her visit that afternoon with Cecily had been fraught with tension. Aunt Katherine had practically sat on top of her the whole time. She hadn't felt free to play with Cecily or give her child much affection without encountering Aunt Katherine's accusing stare.

The mutt made her feel…somehow… accepted.

"Why, Lisa girl, you know I don't mind." Uncle Fred fondled the dog's ears. "I miss my old Scraps more'n I can say. He was more than fine company. Hmm…this mutt is still a pup, I think. Yes, sir, we need to clean her up, and then see where we are."

"Thanks, Uncle Fred." Her heart swelled with pride. She'd praised Uncle Fred's great attitude when she'd told Beth Anne of him, hadn't she? It mattered little that he didn't go to church, or that he was a regular at Benny's Pub several nights a week.

Relieved of her worry, Lisa carried the dog through to the kitchen, setting the mutt on the chipped and crumbling counter near the sink. She kept one hand on the dog's head while she filled a pan of water.

The dog licked her finger. The poor thing was trembling in fright.

"Seems I got a can of dog food somewhere..." Uncle Fred mumbled, hitching up his trousers as he rummaged through his cupboard. "Left over from when I had Scraps."

Lisa crooned as she worked, soothing the dog's occasional whimper, carefully washing her. "We need some antiseptic, Uncle Fred."

"I'll get it," he remarked, setting the can of dog food beside Lisa. "Poor little mite."

He returned with a bottle of hydrogen peroxide, and while he took an opener to the can of dog food, she daubed the animal's wounds, murmuring softly to calm her. The dog finally settled down some.

"Nothing's broken," Lisa concluded. "But she looks as though she's been on her own a long time."

"Uh-huh." Uncle Fred nodded. "I'll take her along to that vet doctor that hangs out at the senior center. He ain't practicing anymore, but he'll look her over and such. He'll tell me where to get her the shots she needs."

Bless Uncle Fred and his senior center. It was better for him there than Benny's Pub.

The phone rang. Neither Lisa nor Uncle Fred wanted to stop what they were doing, but the ringing persisted.

"I'll get it," Lisa remarked finally. "Here, you hang on to the dog. And thanks again, Uncle Fred." She leaned over to kiss his cheek. "You're…you are one of a kind."

"'Preciate that." Uncle Fred laid a tender, gnarled hand on the dog, and the mutt accepted the gesture with a grateful lick. Uncle Fred set the bowl of food in front of her on the counter.

Lisa chuckled. Uncle Fred knew what to do.

She grabbed the phone. "Hello."

"Hi. It's Ethan."

"Oh, hi, Ethan." Her stomach tightened. Was something wrong? Why else would he be calling so soon? "What's up?"

"How's the dog?" Behind Ethan's voice she could hear the excited voices of the children. "My kids won't go to bed till we've found out about the dog."

Was that all?…

"The dog is just fine. Uncle Fred is taking

care of her. She's—" Lisa turned to watch what was happening in the kitchen. "Eating…um, I should say gobbling, right at the moment. Poor thing, she's so hungry I think we can count her ribs."

"She's eating, huh? Okay. Hold on a minute." His voice faded slightly. "You hear that, kids? The dog is having supper. It's—" He spoke into the phone again. "Are you sure it's a female?"

"Yeah. Uncle Fred says she's a tough little critter."

"Hear that, kids? It's a girl dog and…" He addressed Lisa again. "What's she eating?"

"Dog food. Uncle Fred had some."

"That's good. Kids, the dog is eating her supper. Did you ever have a dog, Lisa? Or a cat?"

"No…" Lisa hadn't, but she'd played with neighborhood pets.

"Uh, excuse me a moment…" Lisa heard his muffled voice admonishing his children. "Now scoot off to bed, all of you. No nonsense about drinks and bathroom visits afterwards. We've stretched the limits tonight."

Lisa listened with amusement to the receding little voices. She caught herself smiling, and wondered just how long it would take to get the kids down for the night, overstimulated as they were.

Her Cecily had never minded bedtime, but she was up at the crack of dawn…

"Guess I gotta go," Ethan said. He sounded as though he hated to end the conversation.

"Is that all? That's the only reason you called?"

"Yeah. Guess it is. The kids were restless, and I…they wanted to know about the pooch."

Lisa recognized a bit of loneliness in his voice. She hadn't known before tonight that he was without a job. Her heart took on another worry. How long had he been unemployed? How was he making it, with bills and doctor visits and school, and groceries…and a million things? He was alone with his three kids all day. How much strain was that on his ego?

She had only one child to worry about…and she had a job. Never mind that she didn't have a home yet. That would come in time.

All of a sudden her gratitude climbed high. She *did* have things to be thankful for. She felt stunned at the thought. *You've been looking after me, as promised, Lord. Thank you, Lord.*

"Well, we're just fine…the pooch and I." Her tone softened. "And Uncle Fred is delighted to have another dog around to fuss with. But tell the children they can call again any time to talk about the dog. It won't bother me or Uncle Fred any."

"Okay. That's fine, I'll tell them. Um, Lisa, you didn't answer about lunch."

She thought about it for all of five seconds. He'd been kind…and he didn't have to know about…anything. But could he afford to take her to lunch?

"All right. Lunch. But we go Dutch treat."

"What do you mean? I can afford lunch." He sounded amused, and his happier tone cheered her considerably.

"Can you? If you're out of work?"

He chuckled. "Honestly, Lisa, I can afford a meal without taking the food from my children's mouths."

"Well…all right. I guess."

"That's great. What's your day off?"

"I'm off on Thursdays after the breakfast rush hour, but I have an, uh, appointment at two that's important. If we make it right on time, I can do lunch."

"We'll make the time fit." His voice was cheery. "Great. Okay, I'll pick you up—"

"No," she quickly interrupted. "I'll…meet you. Just say where."

"All right." He didn't argue and named the place. "I'll say goodnight now."

Later, as Lisa cleaned up the kitchen while Uncle Fred found an old quilt for the dog to sleep on, she thought about how much she had to be grateful for in her life.

*I really do praise You, Lord!*

She hadn't been much different from that homeless mutt when she'd come out of prison. Gratitude toward Uncle Fred for giving her a home made her want to weep. And she could stay as long as she needed to…with only a minimum of rent. When she could pay.

Every paycheck, she put away as much as she could. So far it was little enough.

She'd been broke. All she'd possessed had been sold to pay her attorney and pay back the company. Her car, her apartment furnishings. What little jewelry she'd owned.

There wasn't a hope in heaven that she'd

ever pay back the entire amount. But she thought she'd die trying.

It was her choice, one that she didn't regret. The decision had bought her an early release from prison, but it left her depending on Aunt Katherine and Uncle Fred to get started once again.

No one at New Beginnings knew any of that, of course. Except for Beth Anne and Pastor Mike.

And she felt gratitude toward Aunt Katherine for taking in her little Cecily. She was grateful that Cecily had had a decent place to stay during that year and a half. No foster home for her little girl, no sir.

But Aunt Katherine…

What was she to do? Her aunt had hinted again today at keeping Cecily. She wanted permanent custody. Surely she'd been bluffing when she'd mentioned seeing a lawyer.

The trouble was, Lisa had never known Aunt Katherine to bluff about anything. And she'd mentioned the lawyer by name, a Mr. Jenson.

Her resolve stiffened. Lisa would never let her daughter go; as grateful as she was for her aunt's help, she would fight her to the back teeth and bone for her child's custody. But it would cost her—time and money and heartache.

Lisa sighed against her worry.

*Lord, I'll have to trust you…but please let Aunt Katherine see that I'm honestly trying. I will have a home for Cecily, I will. It all takes time…*

She had to quit thinking about it.

"Uncle Fred…" Her thoughts focused determinedly on the days immediately ahead of her.

"Uh-huh." He lifted the dog in his arms and carried her through to the front room. Sitting back down in his chair, he let the little dog settle in his lap. The mutt was asleep as soon as he grew quiet.

She followed Uncle Fred, sinking down on the old couch.

"Next week is Thanksgiving, and…the New Beginnings group is going to have their own celebration on the Tuesday before. We're to bring family. Would you go with me? As my family?"

"Why, sure, honey." The surprise on his face was telling. Had he been neglected in the past by family—by her mom, by her? "I'd be glad to go. But don't you want to take Katherine, so you can have little Cecily there with you?"

"Aunt Katherine won't go, she wouldn't dream of it. I asked her today." Her heart was heavy with the knowledge, and she didn't dare defy her aunt. Katherine had muttered sarcastically that she wouldn't be caught dead at the place before Lisa even finished asking. "And she won't let me take Cecily."

"Now that's a downright crying shame, if you ask me. The selfish old woman, she couldn't have a child of her own, so she's taking over yours. 'Twas fine when you was…er, away…but now you're back, I don't see why you just can't have your daughter without all this folderol. Beats ever'thing, I say. Why, I ought to go over there and tell the old bag a thing or two."

"No, don't. Please. Please, Uncle Fred. It would only make matters worse." She tried to laugh, thinking of Aunt Katherine's tight expression when she thought Lisa was taking advantage of her. But her chuckle was weak.

She sighed then, and said in a low tone, "I'll abide by Aunt Katherine's wishes for a time, Uncle Fred. But the day will come, as soon as I'm financially out from under…you can bet I'll have Cecily then."

Uncle Fred was silent as he watched her, then said, "We gonna name this here mutt?"

"Yeah, you bet." Lisa took a deep breath. Time to change the subject. "How about… Endure?"

"Endure? From what you tell me, she's endured lots. It's a good 'nuff name, I guess. Endure…"

Lisa walked into the posh restaurant where she'd promised to meet Ethan. She wore her best dress, a three-year-old corn-flower-blue with tucks down the front that hid her too-wide hips.

Only Aunt Katherine had ever mentioned her hips being a bit wide. Lisa had been sensitive about them ever since. Never mind… she felt comfortable. She was dressed as nicely as anyone in the restaurant.

Not because she wanted to make an impression. Oh, no… She just wanted…she wanted to…to show him…

Oh, good-night! She did want to impress him.

Frowning, she tucked a strand of auburn hair behind her ear. She spotted Ethan waiting for her with a smile. Smoothing the frown from her face, she greeted him.

"This is nice, Ethan. Have you been here before?"

"Yes, I have," he said as the hostess seated them. "They have wonderful service here and the food is always good. It's a pattern I'd like to copy."

"Copy?"

"Uh-huh. I'd like to have a restaurant myself one day. Didn't I tell you that? I decided last night to go for it, but I've been thinking about it for a while."

She picked up a menu. "Oh. I thought you were a banker."

"I was. But that's not what I'd really like to do." He leaned forward and spoke past the raised menus. "Haven't you ever wanted to change your life, Lisa? Start again? Do something entirely different?"

She stared at him intently. Was he kidding? That was what had brought her to New Beginnings.

"I…am in the middle of doing that now."

"You are? Well, that's just great. You know how I feel then, to want something so badly you'd risk going broke to get it."

The waiter took their order, and they

waited until he had gone to pick up the conversation.

Ethan clearly didn't know what he was getting into, Lisa thought, when he'd told her of his plans. She leaned back against the booth and studied him.

"Ethan, you don't know how chancy opening a new restaurant is. Half of them fail. Or how hard the work is, how expensive. You'd be lucky to break even. Seven days, at all hours. No…." She shook her head. "You just don't know what it's like. Forget it. You'd never survive."

"Why not? I'm a good cook and I know what people like. Besides, food is basic. People have to eat. They love to try a new place."

"There are dozens of restaurants around already, Ethan. So many of them go broke the first year. You'll run your legs off trying to do it all. And after people try your place once, what is there to bring them in again?"

"That something extra, you mean." He fiddled with the silverware. "Hmm…the something extra."

For a moment or two, he seemed to consider the problem, then smiled. "I'll provide a little entertainment, that's what I'll do. I actually have thought it over, and it's what I want to do. I'll form a trio to play during dinner hours on Friday and Saturday nights. Hire a pianist for Sundays. That'll pull the people in."

"Do you have any idea of the cost of all this?" she asked, aghast at his plans. It sounded like a dream left over from youth.

Their food came, and they paused while the server set it down. Lisa tried to think of something she could say to dissuade Ethan, to prepare him for the reality.

"Not totally," Ethan said. "But round about, yeah. And I just…I want to give it a real try, at least. What do you think?"

"I think you're out of your mind, that's what," she said bluntly. She glanced at her salad and took a nibble, savoring the lettuce and fruit combination. "But if you want to find out about the restaurant business, why don't you give it a test run?"

"What do you mean?"

"I mean, do what I do. There's nothing more basic or tiring than being a waitress or waiter. Serving others can teach you humility in a hurry."

Boy, was that the truth. It was an angle she had never considered before. But if Ethan wanted to get to know the restaurant industry, he could learn a lot in a few weeks of real work. "Come work in my restaurant. It's a good chain. They'll hire you for sure."

She threw out the challenge with a provocative tone, never dreaming he'd accept, and took a huge bite of her salad. Minimum wage and depending on tips for a living would teach him a lot.

He studied her, his fork halfway to his mouth.

"Hey! That's not a bad idea. Not bad at all. Who do I contact?"

"You aren't serious?" She'd see him every day?

"Yeah, why not?"

"I wasn't…really, I…"

"Well, I think it's a great idea. I'll apply today."

She felt dumbfounded. He was actually going to do it? What had she been thinking to suggest it?

## Chapter Eight

Uncle Fred actually shaved for the dinner at New Beginnings. He washed his hair and surprised Lisa by wearing a new blue-checked shirt. Out of deference to Lisa and their dinner engagement, he hadn't had a drink all day.

Lisa was rather astonished…he'd gone to so much effort. And for her. It made her think…and made her proud.

She straightened his collar. "You look mighty spiffy, Uncle Fred. Are you trying to impress me, or them?"

"Both, I guess. Don't want you to be embarrassed about taking me along. Have to admit, I'm a mite curious, too. You set such store by these folks."

She let her lashes drop. "I'd never be embarrassed by being seen in your company,

Uncle Fred. Besides, they're just a bunch of people like me."

Not quite. The people at New Beginnings might want a new start in life, but they hadn't served a jail term.

Bitterness rose in her like a gusher. She wished she knew where Rudy had gone. He'd taken her life and twisted it into shreds. If she could only get her hands on him... she'd wring his skinny little neck quicker than you could say splat.

She'd never forgive him. He'd left her to take the blame, escaping with all that money he'd skimmed to some exotic place where he wouldn't be caught. It positively made her teeth hurt to think of him and his wife lounging on a beach somewhere, enjoying that money.

Glancing up, she saw that Uncle Fred was staring at her. Hiding her thoughts should come easier than that, she thought. She'd practiced enough while she'd been involved with that two-headed snake Rudy.

"Come on, Uncle Fred. Let's go."

Despite her earlier conviction, Lisa held her breath when they reached the church. She was fearful some of the people might know Uncle Fred from his rather wild behavior years ago. Or they might think he was unsuitable to be there. Uncle Fred didn't take to church people and church people didn't take to Uncle Fred. They shunned each other, she thought, and his frequent presence in the local bar hadn't helped any. How would he behave now?

He limped into the crowd alongside Lisa with obvious pride. Lisa carried the two bowls of food she had to offer—a seven layer salad and potato salad.

Pastor Michael stood smiling at the front door. "It's good to see you, Lisa. And who have you brought with you?"

"This is my uncle Fred."

"Welcome, Fred. We're so glad to have you." He shook Fred's hand with vigor. No derision shone in his eyes, not a whit. Only kindness. "Hope you enjoy yourself."

Lisa let her breath go and smiled in return as Michael waved a hand toward the gathering. "Go on in. Looks like nearly all of the New Beginners came…the chairs are filling up fast. That salad sure does look good. Don't think we'll go hungry tonight."

Lisa led Uncle Fred down the hall into the multi-purpose room. She stopped by the kitchen to hand over her two salads to Pam, who had organized the vast buffet line.

"Oh, this is good," Pam said with a smile. "We needed more salad."

Scanning the room, Lisa checked to see who else she knew. There was Cassie, who had been so friendly. And that gorgeous creature Samantha whatever—but she never said a word to anyone. Beth Anne, whom Lisa was depending on to make Uncle Fred feel welcome, was working at the far table.

They headed in that direction, and Lisa made the introductions.

"So you're Uncle Fred," Beth Anne greeted with warmth. Lisa relaxed. "I've heard so much about you. I'm so glad to meet you. You've been more than supportive to Lisa in…" Beth Anne glanced around her, noting a dark-haired woman whom Lisa didn't know close by, and lowered her voice. "In recent months."

"Why, thank you, ma'am," Uncle Fred replied in surprise. "Wasn't much to do. The girl needed a place to live till she could get on her feet, and she's my niece. I didn't have no problem with that."

"That's a lot, you know. Not everyone would be so generous. Now, why don't you find a table," Beth Anne suggested as someone else approached. "We'll be ready soon."

"Do you need any help?" Lisa asked.

"I don't think so. We couldn't get anyone else in the kitchen now if we used a steam shovel."

Lisa gave the expected chuckle and turned away. She was gazing around the room, when she felt a small body tackle her legs. Tiny arms clutched her.

Glancing down, she saw a beaming Jordan gazing up at her with a warm smile, his hair in his eyes. Instinctively she smiled back and Lisa placed her hand against his soft cheek. "Why, Jordan, how are you, dumpling?"

"Hi, Miss Lisa."

Lisa looked up to see Ethan coming toward her, Tony and Bethany following. She hadn't seen Ethan since they'd had lunch together.

Tony broke away and skidded to a stop beside her. "How's our puppy?"

"Endure? She's just fine. Eating everyday like she's afraid the food will disappear."

"Does it have fleas?" Tony asked. "The puppy?"

"Not no more," Uncle Fred answered. "We had a vet look her over. She's in fine shape now."

"That's a funny name," Tony said. "We

wanted to name her Tiger. Or Spot, but she doesn't have any spots."

"I wanted to name her Brownie, 'cause she's brown," put in Bethany.

"Well, we named her Endure because she seems to have endured a lot while being lost," Lisa explained to the three little faces gazing up at her. "Do you think Endure will do? She seems to like the name."

"I guess so." Tony was dubious.

"Now don't go pestering Miss Lisa," Ethan warned his brood. "She's not used to children."

Lisa remained silent to let the pain of that remark pass. Her heart squeezed into a little knot. Not used to children?

Then she realized that was too very true… but only because she'd had no chance to be.

"Hi, Lisa." Ethan addressed her directly, his gaze warm and friendly. He hadn't meant to hurt her by the remark. How could he know? "Shall we find a place over there? Those tables are the only ones left with enough space for all of us."

She didn't move. "Ethan, I'd like you to meet my uncle Fred."

"Hi there, Fred. We're pleased to have you come." Ethan held out his hand and Fred took it. Fred made appropriate remarks while the tables filled.

"We'd better sit," remarked Ethan, and led them over to a table for six. "There's over a hundred people here this evening."

Little Jordan sat next to Lisa. She was pleased and bent down to ask him, "Are you hungry?"

"Uh-huh." He nodded and gazed up at her with his great wide eyes. Her heart, admittedly, was a goner.

"Why can't I sit with Courtney?" asked Bethany.

"Because we're having a family dinner," answered her father. "Anyway, I don't think Courtney is here tonight."

"But you let me on Sundays."

"That's different. This is dinner. And I only let you sit with her in church because I know her mom will make sure you don't talk too much."

Bethany sighed and stared solemnly at Lisa, her expression a mixture of irritation and sadness. "We don't have a mom anymore. I don't get to do anything fun."

Was the child saying that to gain sympathy?

Lisa pulled back in shock at the judgment

in the question. The child had been what—barely five when her mother died? Of course she missed having a mother.

She glanced at Ethan. He was listening to Uncle Fred and hadn't heard Bethany. What was his discipline like? Was he too harsh or too lenient? Did he favor the boys?

Ethan was too easy, hands-down, Lisa figured. But this little girl got left out sometimes, probably unbeknownst to her dad.

Lisa leaned closer to Bethany and spoke softly. "I know that you don't have a mom…that your mom has gone to heaven. It's a shame, if you ask me, that you don't have another girl in your house to be on your side. I'm sure your mother was a lovely woman, and you miss her. But you know, even grown-ups don't get to do all the fun things they want to. That's one reason why we have New Beginnings, to work with people who…"

Lisa couldn't believe what was coming from her own mouth. She stared into Bethany's eyes. They'd glazed over.

"Never mind." She patted the child's hand. "We'll have fun today."

Just then Michael, tall and strong, dominating the room by his presence, stood to address the group. Everyone stilled. "Welcome, families. Welcome. We at New Beginnings are so blessed by your presence tonight. This is the first annual Thanksgiving for us, and we hope to have many more."

He paused and gazed about the room. "Let's bow our heads and give thanks."

His prayer was short. *"Oh heavenly Father, we thank You for gathering so many souls here tonight. We thank You for brothers, sisters, sons, daughters, and parents...aunts and uncles...who gladly join us to celebrate our lives in You.... We thank You for this food and for guiding New Beginnings in every step we take...let it be for Your glory. We pray in Your Name...Amen."*

The crowd was silent for five seconds, then people got up from their seats and lined up at the food table, chatting warmly with one another. Lisa and Uncle Fred edged their way along, followed by Jordan and Bethany, then Ethan and Tony. Lisa found herself greeted by several of the New Beginnings crowd. She felt touched by their friendship, and smiled and returned the happy words.

Her heart lifted. She was having a great time...but she longed for her own little girl, and she wished past wishing that she could have Cecily with her.

Cecily was still on her mind a few hours later when Lisa went to get a broom to help clean up. If her daughter were here, she could run and have fun like the other children, be mothered and hugged by the women in the group. Learn new games and make friends.

Lisa's mood had deteriorated to squat. Helping out would be good for her, keeping her too busy to mind her blues too much.

"Hand me that bucket, too, would you please, Lisa?"

She turned to find Ethan close behind her.

"You're pushing your kids' bedtime, aren't you?"

"Yeah, a bit." He frowned. "Been doing that too much lately. Ah, well. My discipline has gone out the window, as my sister tells me." He shrugged, and leaned his shoulder against the wall. "Gotta watch it and keep a better schedule. But this dinner was fantastic, wasn't it? I'm so stuffed I don't want another bite for...hours." He grinned and winked at his mild joke.

She handed him the mop he requested.

"Thanks," he said. "Figured since it was my kid who spilled, it was my job to clean up."

"Yeah, that's how I'd figure it," she answered. But she smiled when she said it.

"I really like coming here, don't you? It isn't just worship, though that's the usual primary activity of a church. I like that well enough and I feel God's presence. But the activities that Michael is planning for this group…"

"Uh-huh. They should go well with the crowd."

He shook his head. "If even half of them come about, there's bound to be growth for the church. And for New Beginnings. I'm coming to feel this is a real family…or like family."

She didn't answer. Was it like a family? She supposed for some it was, those who attended every function. But for her…how would these people feel if they knew all she wanted was revenge…wanted it so badly she could taste it.

It wasn't *all* she wanted, she reminded herself. But sometimes the need for revenge overwhelmed her with enough emotion to choke out other desires.

"That's what it seems to be for some," she said mildly. Who could discount that? She started to close the closet door.

"I guess I'm one of those people. But that's not a bad thing."

"No, of course not. But New Beginnings can't make up for…"

She bit down on her lip.

"Make up for what, Lisa?" His eyes were curious.

"Nothing. Only the past." She turned away from him and started back toward the kitchen. The making up was *her* job. She didn't want only revenge. She honestly wanted to get her life back…and straightened out. She wanted to make a nice, stable home for Cecily and be the best mother she could.

Nothing like the neglectful mother she'd had, nor like her overbearing aunt and all her rules.

Ethan pushed himself away from the wall and hurried to keep up with her. He pulled on her arm. "Lisa…"

She stopped and shook her head. "Never mind me. I'm just feeling a bit…blue today." She tried to smile. Tried, but her mouth trembled. "I'll…I just, oh, I don't know, but I'll…"

She trailed off, stared at him a second, then turned her head away.

"Oh, Lisa." Ethan's compassion grew. He'd felt just this sort of despair after his wife died. "I don't know what you're feeling blue about, but that's the point, isn't it? That's what we come here for? Hope. Encouragement. We can do nothing about the past, but we can do something about *now*, choose how we make the future. We have to move on. With God's help, we can."

Lisa felt a streak of hopelessness. How could she change the things she wanted to change? "We can't choose everything we want. Some things are chosen for us, then we have to deal with them."

"Like what?"

She didn't answer. He folded his hands around her shoulders. He wished she'd look at him. She seemed defeated in some way. Her lashes remained lowered.

Defeated? It wasn't an attitude he'd attribute to Lisa Marley. He continued to talk.

"That's true, Lisa, we can't have everything we want. But we can choose our attitude about the stuff that happens to us." She still had her head turned, and he realized something specific was bothering her. Where was the feisty Lisa? The one with the sassy lip? "What's bugging you, Lisa? What's the matter, hon?"

"Nothing."

"It's something." He wanted to give her a little shake, but he knew that would elicit nothing. "If you don't want to tell me, or to talk about it, you don't have to. It's all right. But you have to talk to somebody." He bent down to peek at her face. "Maybe Beth Anne, she's a good listener. It'll eat you alive till you do. Promise you'll talk to someone?"

She suddenly drew in a deep breath as though she was drawing in her life force. She swallowed, and at last she turned toward him, but her lowered lashes hid her eyes. "Yeah, you're right, I suppose."

He relaxed a bit and lifted her chin so he could see her face better. "Promise me you'll talk to Beth Anne?"

She nodded and looked up at him. Tears glimmered on her lashes. Her mouth drooped, as though she was a breath away from letting the tears flow. He brushed his thumb across her lips, feeling the soft texture.

"Yes, I promise."

He wanted to kiss her. It wasn't only the

sympathy he felt. Long-forgotten feelings buzzed along his veins. "Good."

His mouth lowered to hers. The kiss was warm and soft. She gently returned his pressure. He rested there a moment, feeling his own need grow. He could get lost here... could spend a long time learning her curves and dips. He wanted to take the kiss deeper, but from the reception hall, voices grew louder. He recalled where they were.

Breathless, he slowly withdrew and let her go. She hadn't fought his kiss...she'd welcomed it.

When she returned his stare, she looked as though she'd hit a brick wall. Good! At least the depressed look was gone.

"We'd better go back before they send someone to search for us," he murmured. Her eyes glowed warmly. "Besides, the kids will probably have Uncle Fred tied to a chair if we don't."

Lisa laughed shakily. Her thoughts were jumbled, but she cleared her mind enough to say, "Not your kids..."

"Huh, you'd really laugh if you only knew..."

She though about what Ethan had said a few minutes ago. He was right. She had to concentrate on one thing at a time, and for now that was making a home fit for her child. She'd fight for that as long as she drew breath.

Then she could concentrate on finding Rudy. Or forget about him entirely.

The dinner party was disbanding. Lisa could see Uncle Fred waiting for her in his old truck, slumped down and half asleep. The parking lot held about half the cars it had earlier. Lisa supposed New Beginnings' first strictly social event was a success.

Beth Anne spoke in a low tone as they walked out to the truck. "I'm so glad you brought your uncle, Lisa. He seemed to enjoy the dinner. But I'm sorry you couldn't bring your little girl."

The old saying "sharing troubles cuts them in half" came to mind. Beth Anne knew how much she missed Cecily. She supposed that was why talking to her always made Lisa feel better.

"Oh…" It felt so good to speak of her child to someone. To voice hopes and dreams to someone who was kind and had an open heart.

Before they'd headed out to the parking lot, Lisa had caught a few minutes alone with her friend. Beth Anne had expressed her keen disappointment over not having her daughter with her, and Lisa had felt consoled.

"I suppose I shouldn't count on Aunt Katherine just yet to trust me," she said now. "I…" She bit her lower lip. "I have to prove myself for longer."

She thought of Ethan, too. Three kids, no wife, and now jobless. How did he cope?

Ethan's kiss remained with her. She was sure he'd meant only to comfort her, but she didn't suppose Beth Anne would care to hear about *that*. It was something she'd think about when she had time…. Something to go to sleep on….

Ethan sat across from Mac, the young manager of the Blue Bird Café, the restaurant where Lisa worked.

"You don't have any restaurant experience, huh? Not even while in college or high school?"

"Nope. Not a whit."

Mac doodled a bit on the paper in front of him. "Well, you're way overqualified for this job, you know. And if we hire you, it'll be for the kitchen. Any objections?"

Ethan shook his head. "None at all. I want to learn everything, so I might as well start at the bottom."

"Hmm…our pot scrubbers are pretty young. Do you mind working with teens?"

"Might be fun. Their spirits are usually so high."

"All right. You're hired."

## Chapter Nine

"I did it. I got a job in the same restaurant you work in." It was barely dawn, but calling Lisa to tell her his news had been Ethan's waking thought.

He leaned back against his headboard and crossed his bare feet, running a hand through his hair. It was getting too long, and he'd have to get it cut for work. Half grinning, he felt jubilant, as though he'd achieved something great.

Last night his sister had neatly bawled him out for taking such a low-paying job, but Ethan had paid her no mind. Sisters were sisters.

Now, friends… He held the phone close to his ear and waited for Lisa's reaction.

"Ethan, it's five-thirty in the morning! Did

you call simply to tell me you got hired at the Blue Bird Café?" Her voice sounded softly sleepy…purring into the phone.

He felt the buzz of her voice along his spine. It affected him more than he'd been willing to admit, until after that kiss, which he could still feel in his toes.

He obligingly wiggled them, recalling the powerful emotions that kiss had evoked.

"Yeah. I didn't wake you, did I? I knew you'd be getting ready for your shift."

Her voice sounded muffled. "Yes, I am… but I hope you didn't wake Uncle Fred."

"Oh." Somehow he'd thought only of Lisa. His guilt, however, was light. "Sorry about that," he whispered, losing some of his enthusiasm.

"You really did get the job?" she asked it in wonder.

Hadn't she believed him when he said he wanted to own a restaurant? He guessed she hadn't. He was pretty sure she didn't think of him as a dignified banker either, but simply a guy with three kids.

Ex-banker, he reminded himself. Well, Lisa didn't know him well. Something he wanted to change.

"When do you work?" she asked. "I mean, what shift?"

"Oh, nights for now." He hesitated a moment, glancing at the time. "Hey, I gotta go. Gotta get the kids up for school."

Only Jordan was up. He watched Jordan run his trucks over the floor beside his bed.

"Night shift, huh? You can't leave…I mean, who will look after your kids?"

"It's a problem, all right." He pursed his lips. "I have to have someone willing to stay at night. My young cousin, Georgie Dene, said she'd do it for now."

Georgie Dene had said she'd help out for a little while and not for the whole winter, but he wasn't going to worry about that now. He'd find a reliable sitter. He *had* to find *someone.* "I start tonight."

"That's…great." Lisa's voice brightened a little. Enough to make his spirits soar. "Welcome to the Blue Bird Café, Ethan. I hope you won't be disappointed. What will you be doing?"

"Oh, just kitchen work for now. But you wait. I can make that work for me. I'll learn everything they have to teach me. I'll move up so fast it'll make your head swim."

"I'm sure. Well, I get off at three…"

"And I come on at three."

"So I guess we'll see each other in passing."

"Yeah." If he went in early, he'd manage to have a few moments with Lisa. That would do for now.

His one disappointment was that he'd miss Bethany and Tony when they came home from school. He'd just miss their bus. He'd become used to being there and hearing about their day, and their interaction was important to him.

But they liked Georgie Dene, he reasoned. She was in college and young enough to play with them. He'd told them last night that he was going to work, and they expressed excitement that Georgie Dene was coming.

"So I guess I'll see you later." He grinned into the phone. "Be good till I get there."

"Ethan…I have to be good. There's no other way."

"I'm counting on that. Okay. See you at three."

No other way… Why would she say that? The lessons from New Beginnings were getting to her, he guessed. They'd talked of walking the narrow path of faith last week.

He swept Jordan up and hugged him. "Let's have breakfast."

"'Kay." Jordan grinned at him. "Can I have purple jam?"

"You bet, big guy. Purple jam coming up."

It seemed ridiculous to be so happy about the restaurant job, but he'd been sitting on his duff for too long. Action, that's what he needed. Going back to work felt great!

He wouldn't need all those suits in his closet—much to his in-laws' chagrin. As it was, they figured he'd have been a natural screw-up without their daughter's influence, and now they were waiting for him to need their help. He suspected they wanted to exert more influence on him since Sharon's passing than he'd let them. They must be frustrated as all get out.

Well, this job would annoy them more, but he couldn't help that. The restaurant was as far away from banking as he could get. He took delight in that.

Which reminded him. He ought to check his accounts. He wasn't as low on money as his sister feared, but he should look at his financial situation anyway. See just where he stood. There was enough money for about another year, he figured, if he didn't fritter it away.

He set out cereal, bowls, spoons and milk.

A few minutes after six-thirty, he woke Tony and Bethany. Then he popped bread into the toaster and pulled out the butter and jam, all the while whistling under his breath.

Getting his kids ready for school was routine by now. He was pretty good at it.

Once, he'd left it to his wife to take care of. Sharon had been the one to set out breakfast…and get lunch…and cook and clean up after dinner…and see the kids dressed properly for school.

He let out a gusty sigh. Yeah, he'd had to learn to take care of the kids, not just play with them a bit when he came home for the day or take a turn walking the floor with them at night. It hadn't been easy, but his children had been his salvation, too. They'd needed him.

They'd been the impetus for his joining New Beginnings.

Since his job ended five months ago, he'd slopped around in his pj's till noon, lived in his jeans all afternoon and evening, and learned how to be a full-time dad. He'd had to let go of his babysitters and housekeepers.

And even that delighted his soul, he discovered.

Now that he'd made so many changes in his life and his outlook, he was ready to work again. He was also glad he'd made the move to a smaller house. It suited him better and was easier to keep, and he'd put down a healthy amount so his mortgage payments would be lower to accommodate his single salary. Too many memories at the old place, he'd told everyone, and that was true enough. But also, he didn't want the expense.

He'd cancelled his membership in the golf club, and most of his credit cards, too.

As it turned out, those were wise decisions. He couldn't have gone on supporting those expensive habits. He'd have lost the large house eventually when the merger had lost him his banking job and he couldn't make payments. He'd been a vice-president. His reputation was excellent and he knew he could find a job elsewhere in banking…if he'd wanted it.

That was the trouble. He didn't care if he ever saw the inside of a bank again.

He glanced at his watch.

"The bus is due in five minutes, kids," he called from the front hall.

He took the pink jacket and the dark blue one from the closet and held them out wide while Tony and Bethany slipped into them.

He tucked Bethany's pink scarf tenderly around her neck.

Lord, how he loved them…

"Got your homework, Bethany?"

"Uh-huh."

"Got your homework, Tony?"

"Daaad… I don't have any homework. I'm in kindergarten."

"Oh, that's right, I forgot," he teased. He kissed them each on the nose, then guided them toward the front door.

"Be right back," he yelled at Jordan. He stood on the front stoop with the door open and watched while the kids raced for the bus. Jordan came to stand beside him, hugging his leg. Luckily the bus stopped one door down, and he could observe them get on from here.

Karen Bailey stood with her kid, a big boy for his age. She turned to wave at Ethan and sent him a bright smile.

He gave a little wave, but only to acknowledge her, nothing flirtatious. In his experience, she didn't need any encouragement and her kind could be trouble.

The kids climbed aboard the bus, looking back to give a last wave. As the bus rolled away, he swiftly turned to go into the house.

Karen Bailey called out, "Hi there, Ethan.

My, it's a brisk morning. I could use a cup of coffee about now."

"Sounds good. Um, gotta go, Karen." He swung Jordan up into his arms. "Gotta…"

He slipped through his door, shutting it, then peeked around the edge of the living-room curtain. His neighbor went down the street, decidedly disappointed.

Whew! That was a close one. He'd been friendly when he first moved in, but now found his time more precious.

He set Jordan down to watch some educational children's programming on television, then got out his guitar, sank down on the sofa and tightened the strings.

He plucked idly while his mind wandered, going over his plans—dreams, really—to run his own restaurant. But now was the time to make them a reality.

He strummed a few bars on a new ditty he was working on, but the piece just wasn't coming together.

What was wrong with him today? He felt as antsy as a bug on a Fourth of July pie.

He got up, putting the instrument aside. "Hey, Jordan, where is that drawing pad your sister got for her birthday? Daddy wants to borrow a couple of sheets."

"Back there." Jordan, still watching the TV screen, pointed toward the bedrooms.

Ethan went rummaging. He found the pad under Bethany's bed. Getting out a couple of sheets, he retrieved pencils from the huge desk against the living-room wall and sharpened them. He cleared the dining-room table and put the paper and pencils there. Then he went in search of a ruler.

"Now…"

He worked steadily for the next couple of hours. At one point he went back for more paper, then stopped to get Jordan some orange juice and toast, and distractedly answered a sales telephone call. Other than that, nothing broke his concentration.

Until Tony came home from kindergarten. Ethan heard the bus approaching down the street. Was it that late? He dashed out to meet the bus, taking a half-dressed Jordan with him.

"Daddy, why is Jordan wearing his pj bottoms?"

"Is he?" Ethan turned around and looked at his youngest child. "So he is. Um, guess he was out of clean jeans. I've been busy, but I'll put in a load of wash as soon as we have lunch."

"I'm hungry," Tony announced as they walked into the house. "Can I have peanut butter and jelly?"

"Me, too," Jordan repeated.

"What? Jordan, you had toast in the middle of the morning. You must be growing. You suppose you'll grow as tall as a giant?" Ethan teased as he guided the boys into the kitchen.

"Remember I told you I'm going to work today at the same restaurant as Miss Lisa?"

Tony gazed at him hopefully. "Can we eat there all the time?"

"Nah, not all the time. But once in a while wouldn't hurt. Do you mind that I'm going to work?"

"I guess not. If Lisa's there…"

His kids had taken to Lisa, obviously. So had he.

He was in the middle of spreading peanut butter on a piece of bread when that thought shoved its way through.

He stopped spreading and stared into space for a full minute, the peanut butter standing up in swirls on his knife. Why? Why did he like Lisa Marley so much?

This was nothing like the way he'd felt when he fell in love with Sharon.

But he was older now. And Lisa was…there was something about Lisa that appealed to him. He wondered about her, worried about her, and he somehow thought that was a little funny. He hadn't worried about anyone but his kids and himself since he'd become a widower.

But had he ever really *worried* about anyone before? If she just wasn't so mysterious about her past.

He shook off his feelings. He had enough to think about if he wanted to open a restaurant. He needed to go in to see Andrew Beck about a loan, for one thing. He knew Andrew from the old days. Andrew wouldn't view his proposal as silly or total nonsense. Ethan would take in his rough sketch and see what Andrew made of it.

Ready to leave for work, Lisa glanced at her watch. She had time to run by to see Cecily for a few moments if she left right now.

"Uncle Fred, I'm taking the truck."

He grunted "okay." He didn't need the truck today, he'd insisted. He'd probably go back to sleep, with Endure curled beside him, but she wanted him to know she was leaving the house. Dear Uncle Fred. She hadn't known he was so kind until she'd found herself in all this trouble.

She had a couple of months before she'd be clear of it. The legal side of it. But the emotional price... She supposed she'd be paying for that her entire life.

But if God could forgive her...shouldn't she forgive herself? That was the question she'd been wrestling with these last months. Talking with Beth Anne had helped.

Ten minutes later, she sped by Aunt Katherine's house. Lisa let her breath go; there was a light on in the kitchen. She turned the car around at the corner and parked at the curb in front.

Knocking softly, she waited. She had to improve matters with her aunt or she would never win her over, Beth Anne had told her. Lisa knew her friend was right. Her visits had been strained and tense, and if they continued in that way...

Last week Beth Anne had asked her why she'd left Cecily with Katherine in the first place, since they didn't seem to get along. Lisa had told Beth Anne about the years she and her mother had spent with Aunt Katherine. How she'd rebelled against the very strict rules her aunt had imposed.

At times, Lisa wondered at her decision herself. But when the whole mess with Rudy came down, she was in a state of confusion. The terrible hurt and rage she'd experienced when she'd discovered Rudy's duplicity had left her overwhelmed. She'd been alone, terrified and helpless, and afraid Rudy might want Cecily in spite of what he'd told her. And no way had Lisa wanted her child in foster care. Aunt Katherine's home was the only one she knew where Cecily would be protected and safe.

For that she was profoundly thankful. Aunt Katherine *had* taken Cecily in and provided a home for her. Lisa reminded herself of that once more as Uncle Mark came to the door.

"Lisa. Is anything the matter?"

"No, no." She offered a tremulous, tentative smile, and pushed the troubling thoughts behind her. "I merely wanted to see Cecily before I go to work this morning. I have only ten minutes to spare."

"She's still in bed." He opened the door.

"Who is it, Mark?" Her aunt called from the bedroom. She came into the living room as Lisa walked into the house. "Oh. It's you. What is it, what do you want?"

"Nothing, Aunt Katherine. I only wanted to say hi before I start my morning shift." She peeked through to the tiny bedroom at the back of the house.

Just then the little girl appeared at the bedroom door, rubbing her eyes, still in pink footed pajamas.

Lisa's heart smiled, and she glanced at her aunt. The sour look on her aunt's face couldn't ruin this spontaneous visit. She'd be *very* pleasant.

"There she is." She went down on her haunches and held out her arms while Cecily walked into them. Little Cecily felt sweeter than pure sugar. How could she ever let her go? "Hi, sweetheart. I can't stay long, but I came by to say how much I missed you."

"Can you play with me?" Cecily asked.

Lisa held her daughter tightly for a moment, not wanting to let go, wanting to keep her there forever, then reluctantly released her. "Not this time, baby. But I'll play on Thursday, I promise."

"You'll be late for your job, won't you?" Aunt Katherine asked. Hand on her hip, her stance said "leave." "What are you doing here, anyway?"

"How are you, Aunt Katherine? Is your arthritis any better today?"

Automatically, the older woman rubbed her right hand, though she denied her pain. "I'm fine. Don't think you can run in and out at will, my girl. I've seen my lawyer again, and he said to be firm about visits. Did you want something specific?"

Lisa compressed her lips, then forced them to relax. "Seeing my daughter isn't specific enough?"

Katherine frowned. "Well, you're constantly breaking the visitation rules."

"I only wanted to see Cecily before the long day started." Lisa suppressed her irritation before it showed, then sighed. She kissed the soft cheek once more and stood to leave. "I have to be going now, sweetie. You be a good girl for Aunt Katherine, you hear? Mommy will come again soon."

She turned to go. Her aunt could make all the threats she wanted to, toss out all the snide remarks and innuendos she could muster, but Lisa would have her daughter back as soon as she'd saved enough for a down payment on an apartment.

And she'd do it without any more outbursts at Aunt Katherine even if it made her choke.

"Don't come unexpectedly again, Lisa, or I'll report you. You have no right to come."

On her way out, Lisa turned. "I *am* Cecily's parent, Aunt Katherine. You can't keep me from seeing her."

"But you aren't the only one, are you? There are other people to consider. Others who have Cecily's best interests at heart."

"What do you mean by that? Cecily's welfare is precious to me. I'm working hard…"

"Yes, but how long will that last? And what if you are? How much will that provide?"

"I don't know, but it'll be the best of what I have. And when I can, I'll take Cecily home to live with me."

"Not if her father shows up!"

"He wouldn't do that. He isn't at all interested in Cecily. He *couldn't* come home and not be arrested."

"Oh, no? Well, maybe not. Maybe not. But he can sign adoption papers, to my way of thinking. He can sign anything he wants to."

"You'd have to find him first, Aunt Katherine. You'd have to prove paternity. That takes money."

"Hmph!" But there was a victorious light

in the older woman's eyes, and she spat out, "Money! We'll see…"

Surely her aunt didn't know where Rudy could be found. Why, she didn't even know Rudy! Didn't know how Rudy dealt with people.

No, Aunt Katherine was only making trouble.

# Chapter Ten

Lisa had already changed from her waitress uniform, getting ready to go home, when Ethan walked into the back room to put on the uniform his boss had just given him. He grinned at Lisa.

"Hiya, Lisa."

"Hi, yourself." She tipped her head and squinted at him. A slow smile spread across her face. Ethan was always so positive about things. "Are you sure you want a job like this?"

"Sure I do. Why do you ask?"

"Oh, I'd have thought you'd want to go back to banking. No one spills food and everyone talks nice to you. Clean clothes, polite people. Easy working conditions."

"Easy? You think banking is easy?" He

said it teasingly and raised a brow. "Only if you really like that sort of thing. People are pretty much the same everywhere in my opinion. Polite and businesslike or cranky and demanding. The people here seem nice enough."

He slid his keys into his pocket and patted them.

"And I hope these working conditions teach me how to cook in bulk, buy in bulk, what suppliers to use and how to offer excellent service. I want to see if my ideas are workable, if they're even feasible."

Lisa watched him slip on his apron and cap for his first shift as she prepared to leave.

"I didn't mean the people here weren't nice." She shrugged. "But you know, they are… Well, a lot of older people come here, lots of families, and you want to be extrapatient."

"Oh, I don't see why that makes a difference. Or how, exactly. Service in a restaurant seems no different to me from service in a bank. Service is service, I would think. It's only the product that has changed. Besides, I won't meet the public because I'll be in the kitchen."

"You think so, huh?"

"Yes, I do. Say, Lisa…are you upset about something?"

"No…it's just…I can't…" She turned away from him, and he reached for her arm.

"Something's bothering you." His fingers tightened. "What is it? Maybe I can help."

His hand felt more comforting than she'd imagined. But she couldn't depend on him. She mustn't. She glanced at him, staring right into his dark eyes. Why worry him? He had enough to be concerned about.

"Nobody can help. I have to find a way to…I can take care of it myself, don't worry. Never mind."

"A shared burden is only half a load to carry."

Lisa remembered thinking the same thing after she'd talked to Beth Anne the night of the Thanksgiving dinner.

"How were your kids when you left them today?" she asked.

Startled at her switch in conversation, Ethan frowned. "They were fine. Why?"

"Did they want you to leave?"

"They didn't mind it. I told them I had to go back to work sometime, so they know that I'll be away for a bit. I've been home too long—every day, in fact, for the last few months. They're too used to me. Besides, they have my young cousin Georgie Dene to play with and they love her. She's agreed to watch them for the time being."

"That's nice." She was silent a moment. "Was little Jordan upset at all?"

"Nah. He knows I'll see him in the morning." His forehead wrinkled. "What is all this anyway? Do you think I'm neglecting my kids?"

"No, of course not." She tried to turn away.

"Then what is it, Lisa? Come on—" he shook her arm "—don't tell me 'nothing' again. It *is* something. Something is troubling you. I've seen you at the meetings when you think no one is paying attention. You've been moping for weeks now."

"Well, I…"

The concern in his eyes told her she had a willing listener, one who would be sympathetic. She was sorely tempted. "Okay. Can I trust you?" At his frown, she blinked and said quickly, "Yes, yes I can. Of course, I can. I didn't mean anything, it's just…I can't trust everyone, you know?"

"You can trust me, Lisa. Now what's the matter?"

"I haven't told you, but I—"

"Haven't told me what?"

She moistened her lips and began again. "I have a little girl. Cecily. She doesn't live with me, I...I can't tell you why. She's staying with my aunt Katherine and her husband, Mark." Her voice climbed higher with emotion. "And she gets good care there. The best. I'm not worried about that."

"A child? A little girl? I wasn't aware that you had a kid, Lisa. Didn't even know you were married. Why haven't you mentioned her?"

That was the problem, wasn't it? If she'd been married, she could have told him sooner. Or would that really have made a difference? Discounting the father was common enough in today's world, she thought. Even having a child out of wedlock and not mentioning the father didn't cause a ripple in most people's thinking. It was accepted.

Accepted even by Christians.

She thrust her chin high. If he disapproved, now was the time to find out.

"I'm not married. The father is. But he isn't in the country now, and...uh...I don't expect him to, uh... He doesn't want us..."

Her shoulder twitched. "He wants nothing to do with us, and he doesn't care anything about Cecily. He wanted me to abort her, and when I wouldn't, he took off. I'm sorry I ever became mixed up with him. The circumstances are unusual, though…"

His speculative but sympathetic gaze caused all kinds of defensive feelings to well up inside her, and she rushed on to explain. "I didn't have a choice in the matter. But now I think Aunt Katherine wants permanent custody of Cecily."

"Can she do that? Take custody?"

"Not in the regular scheme of things, no. I'd never give up the right to raise my own child. But there are, or rather were, circumstances beyond my control that I'd rather not—not tell you…just yet…."

She took a breath. Her mouth trembled and she struggled to control her emotions. She glanced down at her hands. They were folded so tightly her knuckles shone white.

"Lisa…" he mumbled in sympathy, and reached for her. She pulled away, refusing to look at him.

"It's difficult. Things will straighten out eventually, I think. I hope, anyway. It's only that I'm working so hard to get things right…"

Deep compassion as well as curiosity stirred Ethan. Lisa didn't want to tell him all that was troubling her, and he suddenly knew it wasn't wise to press her. Now was not the time. But he wanted to know her whole story at some point.

He wanted to kiss her, to nuzzle her neck, to make her feel better... Sliding his arm around her, he was surprised when she tentatively accepted his touch. He began to wonder...what about the child's father? Who was he? Was Lisa still in love with him?

What had caused her to have so little that she'd had to give over her child to her aunt's care? Was she working hard to get her back? Of course she was....

He said the words out loud. "Of course, you are, honey. Nobody's questioning that. What's the problem then?"

"I don't know what to do. I haven't any money, and no home of my own... Everything I had was sold."

"What do you mean it was sold?"

"Um, to pay debts. I have a poor credit history, I'm afraid. I've learned my lessons on that issue, and I'll never allow myself to do it again...you know, abuse my credit cards. But still—"

She straightened away from him, glancing out at the busy activity beyond the door. "You should go, Ethan. You can't be late your first day. It's almost three. And I'm on my way to see Beth Anne. I hope she can give me some direction about…about all this."

"That's a good idea, hon. All right, Lisa. I'll go because I have to. They'll be looking for me. But I'll be thinking of you today. Praying. And hey! Don't worry so much. Beth Anne is good at solving problems. And Mike Faraday, too. If you can't find Beth Anne, talk to Michael. Ol' Mike really knows how to pray, too."

He spoke as though he knew what he was talking about, and he lifted Lisa's chin to gaze squarely into her eyes.

"Yes, I know that's true," she said. "So does Beth Anne. We prayed a lot while I was…" She sniffed and straightened her shoulders. "Well, I will, if I find him. And thanks, Ethan. Thanks a lot. You've helped more than you think you have." She gave a slight smile. "And good luck tonight."

"Thanks for that." Ethan chuckled gently and stiffened his shoulders, too. "My sister thinks I'm totally insane, but here goes."

Lisa left work with an image of Ethan marching off to find the manager as though he were facing a gladiator.

Lisa hadn't made an appointment with Beth Anne, but decided to take a chance she'd be in. Driving past the library, she nearly had a wreck as she slammed on the brakes.

Why hadn't she been to the library yet to use the computers? She could search for that slithery snake Rudy. He'd loved his computer, and she was sure he'd be connected to the Web some way. He couldn't help himself.

And she knew his favorite sites.

The library…not at this moment, she thought as she pressed down on the accelerator again. But soon. If she could only talk to Rudy somehow, she was sure she could lure him back to the States.

Then she'd have him. So would the authorities.

She drove to the church and parked. She couldn't be out too long with the truck because Uncle Fred wanted to use it later. It seemed a bit strange to see the church lot nearly empty. She thought back to the first night she'd attended New Beginnings.

She could admit it now. She'd been scared out of her wits that night. But that was weeks ago, and she'd gained a lot of confidence since then. And friends. Including Ethan... The church felt familiar and comfortable.

Yeah, right. As comfortable as a pair of brand-new shoes. But with wearing, shoes could become comfortable.

A recent model car sat in the parking lot. She thought it was Michael's. She didn't see Beth Anne's car.

Should she leave? Her immediate reaction was to get out of there as fast as she could. But then, that was the old pattern, wasn't it? The pinch of the tight shoes? Never quite facing the ugly realities?

Running away would never solve her problems.

She spoke aloud, hoping God would hear her prayer.

*"Okay, God. I'm here again, needing help. Your help, and a lot of it, because Aunt Katherine won't listen to anyone else, and she thinks of only Your stern commands. She hasn't learned about Your love yet. And I'm not sure what she's got, but it sounds like she has an ace in the hole. I've got to talk to somebody about it... So here goes."*

She recalled Michael's kindness…and Ethan's encouragement.

She took a deep breath, got out of the truck, and marched into the church. She found Michael in the office. A secretary was just leaving.

"Hi, Michael." She gazed about her, a little lost. His office was piled high with books. "Can I, um, talk to you a minute? I usually talk to Beth Anne, but…."

"Ah… I'm sorry she's not here. Beth Anne had a slight emergency with another church member. Come in, come in." He indicated an office chair, one that looked well-used. "Here, take that chair. It's more comfortable."

That word again…*comfortable.*

She lowered herself slowly. Biting her lip, she stared at her lap. She'd worn dark-green slacks today, with a matching green sweater. She'd bought them more than three years ago, but luckily, the style was timeless. She knew green was a good color for her—it made the red appear in her hair.

"What can I do for you, Lisa?"

She glanced up. Michael's eyes invited her to tell him what was on her mind. She cleared her throat. "You know about me, don't you? My…prison term?"

"Yes. Beth Anne told me." His eyes were steady. And kind. She saw no condemnation there.

She nodded automatically. "I figured as much."

"How are you getting along at home?"

"Fine."

"Your Uncle Fred seems nice." He leaned back. "I enjoyed talking to him."

"Did you? I'm so glad. Uncle Fred is… well, he sometimes…often in fact…well, he drinks a little. I was afraid…"

"Hmm…" Michael didn't show surprise. Maybe he already knew that, too? "But he wasn't drinking the day of our Thanksgiving party, was he?"

"No, he wasn't," she replied with gladness and not a little pride. "He refrained for me, I think. Thanks for asking about him." She hesitated "Pastor…"

It was the first time she had addressed him in such a way, but it was as a minister that she needed him. "I have a problem…."

She began to talk, and it was as though a dam had burst. She talked and talked. Her story came pouring out, how she'd gotten mixed up with Rudy… "I was lonely, and my life wasn't…that is, I'd broken up with a boyfriend who was a stinker and going nowhere…seems like I can't pick good men.…"

She explained how she became involved with Rudy's schemes. "I honestly believed him when he said his wife was dying, and he needed the money just until the insurance kicked in…"

And then about Cecily…

"It was so stupid, the lies that I believed, and my own carelessness and utter disregard for—for anyone, I guess, much less myself…or maybe *except* myself," she said with sudden insight. She stopped, registering the thought. "But in the end I had a beautiful little girl. I adore Cecily."

She was silent for a moment. Pastor Michael remained quiet, a slight frown marring his features. "What then?"

"Rudy wanted me to abort her. That was my first clue that he wasn't the man I thought he was. He didn't mean a thing he'd told me. Much less anything he'd promised. He'd lied about everything."

She sighed, feeling ashamed at her own gullibility.

"Do you still love this man?"

"Goodness, no. It wasn't love, was it? I

know that now. Women can be stupid, you know, so…so *willing* to believe only what they want to hear. But I'd give my life for Cecily. I want to see her grow up, to love her, to fix her meals and—and help her join the Girl Scouts, and pick out clothes and—and…I want to teach her how to avoid my mistakes. I want to raise her to know God. He's our Heavenly Father, right? I didn't have a father I could trust either; he left when I was just a little kid. Now I'm learning to trust the fatherhood of God through His Son, Jesus."

"Good for you, Lisa. That's an almighty achievement many Christians haven't yet made."

"And Cecily can, too. She's mine, don't you see? My only chance to have a child. I— I'm nearly past the age of childbearing, you see. Forty, my last birthday."

"That's not old, Lisa. You have a lot of life yet to live."

She nodded. "Yes, I feel that way. I feel if I can raise Cecily the right way…not the way I grew up…I'll be satisfied with my life. And now Aunt Katherine is making threats to keep her."

"That's the problem, hmm?" Michael

asked. "You're sure Rudy wants no part of Cecily?"

"No." She shook her head. "Not a particle. Shortly after the money came up missing, he disappeared. And his wife, too. As you know, I was prosecuted."

"You have no idea where he is?"

"I suspect he's on a Caribbean island somewhere, or in Mexico. He always loved warm weather." She leaned forward. "I'd like to find the son-of-" She stopped the curses forming in her mind.

"Sorry." Drawing a deep breath, she continued. "I suspect the police would like to know, too. But right now I can't let anything get in the way of my regaining Cecily. But what should I do about regaining Cecily? Uncle Fred's house isn't a good one to bring Cecily into; he's a dear and all, but he…he drinks. The rooms are tiny, and there are only four of them. And I can't move in with Aunt Katherine. She'd want to control my entire life." And Lisa would hear about her sins and shortcomings each day. "Her home is tiny, too. Besides, she wouldn't allow it, plus my life would be a living hell…."

"Sorry," she mumbled again.

"Mmm…" Pastor Mike was quiet for a

while. He'd leaned back in his chair and was toying with his pen. "How's your job?"

"It's okay so far. Nothing to brag about. It's steady, though, and I plan to keep it until I can see a way to something better."

"All right. You sit tight, and I'll see what I can do with your aunt. I can call on her at least. Sometimes that does the trick."

"Oh, will you?" Lisa was elated and grateful. She hadn't imagined he would go see Katherine. "That would be wonderful. She is so difficult with me, but she'd be nicer to a minister. She respects the profession anyway. And you can meet my Cecily."

After Lisa left, Pastor Mike thought he ought to make the visit to her aunt right away. He knew the neighborhood where she lived, and he could make a stop on his way home. It was only… He shrugged his disappointment away. He'd been hoping he'd get a call from his wife Rina.

A friendly call.

He thought about his own situation as he drove to visit Lisa's aunt.

*Oh, Lord, I am so sorry for the grief I caused Rina and the rest of the family. I know they are disappointed in me. Give me the*

*chance to make it up to them...please...
please.*

Then again, he supposed Rina had every right to be angry with him, but he missed her pretty, expressive face like mad. And his children. More to the point, he didn't like being separated from them. Look at where it often led. Lisa was another example of a family without a father...

He should practice what he preached.

*I will trust in You, Oh Lord, with all of my heart, with all of my being...for the rest of my life.*

He let out his breath as he found a parking spot on the street a few houses down from the address Lisa had given him. He had to get his mind on the problem at hand—Katherine and Mark...and little Cecily.

At least here maybe he could do some good. Be some help—if he couldn't effect a change in Katherine's attitude, he wasn't sure if Lisa could continue being patient.

## Chapter Eleven

Lisa reached home, tired and thinking of Cecily. Her child didn't have the same freedoms that Ethan's kids did, she mused. Other than preschool, Cecily had no playmates and few outings. Mostly, she wore dresses, old-fashioned ones that were Aunt Katherine's choice. She was only allowed to watch a limited number of television programs, though, and that was okay.

Cecily was kept clean, was fed three meals a day, and had a nice little room of her own. It could be worse.

But mother and child weren't together. Lisa couldn't give her little girl the daily doses of love she wished to give her.

In spite of her worries, Lisa breezed into the house feeling lighter than she had in weeks. Surely, Michael would make a favorable impression with Aunt Katherine. Her aunt respected ministers. She'd be more forthcoming with him, and maybe…just maybe things would improve between her and her aunt.

She could hope, couldn't she?

She'd have a better chance of visiting more often, of taking care of her little girl as she dreamed of doing. In a few months, she'd have enough money saved to get her own apartment. It needn't be large…just in a decent neighborhood. Maybe near a park.

Endure came bounding over to her, and Lisa bent to rub her head. "Hi, girl. How are you, hmm?" The dog licked her hand, and Lisa felt grateful for the affection. "My Cecily will love you, yes she will…"

Uncle Fred came out of his room, dressed for a night out.

"Hi, Uncle Fred." She stood straight, tossing her keys on the end table. "I suppose you're going out tonight?"

"Yeah." He grabbed his brown wool jacket from the coat tree. "Promised to meet my buddies, Leo and Matt, at Benny's. Haven't seen the boys for a while. They're showing a basketball game on TV."

"Okay." She ducked her head. She felt guilty for using his truck so often. She didn't see any other way to get around, but still, she'd disrupted Uncle Fred's life. "I'll get some supper so you can be on your way. Are burgers all right?"

"Never mind me, Lisa girl. I'll pick up something at Benny's. What will you eat?"

"Oh, I'll find something. It's all right. I've got some reading to do for the Bible Study anyway."

"What are you studying?"

"John...and Hebrews."

"Okay. Well, don't wait up for me." He opened the door with an eager thrust. "I might be late."

She never waited up for Uncle Fred. No telling what time he'd wander home. "No, I won't."

She watched the old man go with mixed feelings in her heart. He'd been hitting the bar less and less since she'd come to live with him, and she'd hoped the new patterns would stick. But she felt a sorrow that he found his friends at the bar and not somewhere else. He'd mentioned a seniors' center, but he didn't go often, as far as she knew. Perhaps she could volunteer there when she had some time, and encourage him to go with her. She only hoped Uncle Fred wouldn't drink more than he could handle tonight.

Doing what was right wasn't always easy, she was finding. She was the first to admit that sometimes it was a struggle. The temptation to find Rudy tugged at her mind constantly. It was a fierce, hot need, seething just beneath the surface. She felt guilty about it, about spending the time thinking about it.

But what he'd done to her was a horrible thing to do to anyone, she reasoned. A crime and a sin. She wanted him to pay. She wanted him to suffer. She wanted to catch him and reap her just revenge.

Which was the worse sin, she wondered? Drinking too much or exacting sweet revenge?

She'd have to ask Michael.

She went into the kitchen and opened the fridge. After looking inside a moment, she closed it.

Why couldn't she start her search for Rudy right now?

She wondered where she could find a ride to the library. She remembered a few user names and passwords Rudy liked. Would the library have a computer available tonight?

Was it worth spending the money on a taxi?

It was. She looked up the number of a cab company in the phone book and punched it in.

The taxi took its time coming, but at last Lisa was on her way to the closest library. She watched the route the cab followed. The library was less than four miles from Uncle Fred's. She could walk home if she had to, Lisa decided.

Once she'd paid the driver, she went inside and inquired about using the computers. They were all in use at the moment, and while she waited for one to be free, she filled out an application for a library card, then wandered the cookbook aisles.

Finally the librarian called her name. A computer was free. Lisa slipped her jacket off and glanced at the clock. She had about fifty minutes until closing. Not long, but long enough to get started.

At nine o'clock when the lights flashed, signaling that the library was about to close, Lisa made a face and turned off the computer. She'd searched a few chat rooms that she knew Rudy liked, but with no luck.

Rising, she put on her jacket. Determined not to become discouraged, she made an appointment to use the computer again, then left.

Yet, as she zipped her jacket closed and stepped away from the library, she felt calmer in knowing that she was doing *something*.

The wind blew down, lifting bits of trash along the street. Turning up her collar, she remembered that her gloves were on the table at home. Her teeth started to chatter. She stuck her hands into her pockets.

She started the long walk home at a good clip. It was very dark at times; she wasn't afraid, but she was grateful that there were sidewalks. Part of her route wouldn't have sidewalks, she knew, and she'd have to walk along the street.

The route carried her past a strip shopping mall with a tavern on the end. She was almost past when she registered the name of the tavern and suddenly slowed. Tons of vehicles were parked in front of it, Uncle Fred's included.

What luck!

It wasn't the usual time Uncle Fred left for home, yet she was sure she could convince him to come now. She rubbed her fist against her cold nose.

Walking up to the door, she hesitated. Then, her mind set, she swung the door open and entered. The room was only half-full, smokey and with the odor of beer in the air. She spotted Uncle Fred at the end of the bar, sitting with two older men. They were watching a basketball game on a big screen.

She hadn't a clue about basketball, but she knew she couldn't expect Uncle Fred to leave the bar and his buddies in midgame just to please her.

Biting her lip, she pondered leaving without saying anything to her uncle. Just as she was about to turn, he spotted her.

"Lisa girl. What's wrong?" He climbed off his stool and started forward.

People turned as he called, and his buddies stared. Oh, my…had she embarrassed him?

"Um, nothing, Uncle Fred. I was at the library and was just going home. I'm sorry to disturb you. It's just that I saw your truck outside, and I, um…"

"You sure nothing's wrong?"

She forced a smile. "Yeah, I'm sure. I didn't realize this was the place you hang out." A loud roar erupted from the bar—their favorite team had scored.

"I'll run on home now," she said. "You get back to the game. Have a good time."

"Now wait a minute, Lisa girl. You walked

all the way to the library? It's about four miles, isn't it?"

"No. I took a taxi. But it isn't too far, and I thought I'd walk home."

"If you'll hang around for about thirty minutes, I'll take you home. No use walking in the dark. It's cold, too."

Hesitating, she fingered her jacket's collar. The bar was warm and cozy. It wouldn't hurt to wait for a little while.

"All right."

She followed Uncle Fred to his end of the bar and seated herself on a stool.

"Fellahs, this here is my niece, Lisa." He nodded to two men about the same age he was. "This is Leo, with a full head of white hair, and that one with no hair is Matt."

"Look who's talking," groused Matt in a friendly way.

"So this is the one who's been keeping you at home? What'll you have, Miss Lisa?" asked Leo, his face creasing into a smile.

"Uh, a cola, I guess." Lisa glanced at the faces around her. These old boys had already had a number of beers. "Um…I'd really like a cup of tea, but I guess that's out."

"No tea at Benny's," Uncle Fred told her. "Have to wait until we get home."

"A cola will be fine," she said. "I appreciate—"

The men in the booths behind them hollered out protests, voicing their dissatisfaction with the referees. "He's blind, I tell ya..."

Lisa giggled and started to relax. It wouldn't be hard waiting the thirty minutes. Perhaps this arrangement could become a regular thing, she mused.

Yeah, regular visits to the library chasing after Rudy would take the edge off her frustrations. She settled down to wait.

By the time Ethan had been at the Blue Bird Café a week, he felt he could take care of the kitchen clean-up in his sleep. He prided himself on seeing that the back corners of all countertops and appliances were clean, and the floor was scrubbed to a high shine. He searched out French fries under the stove, layers of grease and dust. He saw lettuce as it was dropped by a waitress, and the remains of ice cream or pudding spattered over the floor. He scrubbed it all, between putting dishes in the industrial dishwasher and hanging up clean pans.

He took the jokes and teasing of the two

boys at the grill with quick responses that made everyone laugh. He made friends with the chef, and asked enough questions to irritate the guy.

Ethan backed off. A little. But when a new chef came on duty for a five-night run, he asked the same questions again, trying to gain a different perspective. This time the answers came willingly, with explanations of why something was done this way or that.

Ethan ate it up. It jazzed him. He could *do* this.

Come Wednesday, Ethan reminded the boss that he'd be off the next night.

"Sure, I remember," Mac said. "Always Thursdays. Have fun at your meeting."

But there was one problem—Georgie Dene couldn't sit, and by the time she called Ethan to tell him it was too late to get someone else. He wanted to attend New Beginnings. He needed it.

The only solution was to take the kids again.

"Okay, munchkins, you're going with Daddy again."

"Where?" asked Bethany, finishing her macaroni.

"To the church. To New Beginnings."

"Aw, to that?" groused Tony. "Can I take my truck? I get bored."

"Yeah, but we get to stay up late," pointed out Bethany. His daughter was too smart for her own good.

"Hmm, you'd better enjoy it, because it won't happen often." Ethan turned to Tony. "Yeah, I suppose you can take your truck. But you better keep the noise down this time, or it'll go in time out."

"Are we gonna see Lisa?" asked Jordan eagerly.

"Probably." Ethan hoped so, anyway. He stooped down to help Jordan into his coat. He'd hardly seen her at work; she was always on the way out as he came in, and they'd scarcely said anything to each other beyond a hello. He didn't like that part of it. She was beginning to be a must in his life.

Yet she was looking a little happier yesterday, he thought, and he didn't worry so much.

He stopped in the middle of zipping Jordan's jacket. Worried? About Lisa? Why would he worry about her?

"Daddy…"

"Sorry, tiger." Ethan finished zipping the jacket. "Didn't mean to hold you up. Let's hurry now."

He stood and looked at the older two. Bethany already was pulling on her blue knit cap. Tony was stacking coloring books. The children meant the world to him…and some days he more than felt the sharp loss of Sharon…but somewhere in his heart was a crack that Lisa had wedged herself into.

He left his house in a state of mild surprise.

Michael stood welcoming people at the front door. The crowd was bigger tonight, filling more of the chairs. Ethan felt glad to see the increase, and knelt to unpack his guitar.

Lisa was already there, sitting on a seat at the back. Ethan smiled at her, noting the empty chair beside her. Jordan ran to her, and she lifted him to sit on her lap.

Ethan and Jimmy played until everyone was seated and Michael was ready to begin the meeting.

As usual, he opened with prayer, and after the prayer, he stared thoughtfully at his audience for a few moments.

"I'm so glad to see you all tonight," he began at last. "We're approaching the Christmas season. All the decorations are out in the stores, and songs reflect the holiday spirit.

Everyone is shopping overtime. We'll be celebrating the birthday of Jesus soon.

"I've been wondering what we here at New Beginnings should do to celebrate, and I thought—we had a wonderful time at Thanksgiving, didn't we? And for those of you who are new at New Beginnings, I'm sorry you missed it." He breathed deeply. "But do we only want it to be a social gathering?"

His quiet question caught some of the members by surprise. They stared back into Michael's steady gaze and grew quieter.

"No…" murmured a sweet voice into the silence. Cassie Manning, Ethan thought.

A few voices followed hers, then someone asked, "What do you have in mind, pastor?"

Michael smiled in recognition. "Quite right, Lon. I do have something in mind. A family with two children were burned out of their house just down the street last week. Local organizations are doing what they can, but I'm wondering what we can do? What should New Beginnings be responsible for?"

"What do you want us to do, pastor?" asked Bob Warden.

"Who among you lives in this neighborhood?" Michael asked.

Three or four hands went up, and people looked at each other, puzzled.

"I got it," said Pam. "Those two kids… they're in our school district. They need to live here so they can get to school every day."

"That's right."

"You're looking for some place for those kids to stay, aren't you?" asked Cindy Crosby.

"That's right. I know it's hard for some of you to promise to help. The commitment will be for a couple of months. I don't know if you can take the whole family or not, but it would be good to take in the kids at least, so their schooling won't be interrupted."

"It'll be tight, but I guess I can manage," offered a hesitant Cindy. "I think my kids go to the same school."

"All right. I'll see you after the meeting to make arrangements. Now we can't expect Cindy to feed those extra mouths on her own. Who can help with the groceries?"

Several hands rose, and Ken said eagerly. "I'll volunteer. I can shop."

Chuckles erupted. It was commonly thought that Ken would do anything to gain Cindy's good graces.

Ethan saw Lisa's hand slowly go up. He glanced at her. She resolutely faced straight ahead, determination on her face. Then his hand rose, as well.

Lisa had to live with her Uncle Fred to get by, yet she still wanted to help out. He knew she saved every penny she could toward her own apartment, and Ethan suddenly realized how hard that must be for her. He wondered why she didn't have a home of her own. What happened before?

Yet her hand remained up as Michael counted numbers.

Ethan didn't understand all there was to Lisa, but he admired her generosity. If she could contribute something to the grocery bill of a family in need, then he could as well.

A short time later the meeting broke for coffee.

"I've got to get the kids home and in bed," Ethan groused to Lisa. "This getting a baby-sitter is a real problem, sometimes. I see Cindy has her kids with her tonight, too. Maybe we should look into getting a perma-nent sitter here at the church."

"Good idea," Pastor Mike said, overhear-ing. "I've been talking to the church board about the idea. Beth Anne has been pitching it since we began our meetings."

"That would be really great," Barbara Wilkins agreed. "It would make things easier for me, anyway."

"I'll see what I can come up with before next week," Pastor Mike promised.

"Can we have some cake?" asked Tony, coming up beside Ethan.

"Sure," Ethan told his son. "But I think we'll have to take it home with us tonight. Okay, sport?"

"I'll walk out with you," said Lisa.

They wandered out to the parking lot. Ethan put his kids into the car, then walked Lisa over to her vehicle. She got into the old truck, and he lingered against her window to say good night.

"Say, Lisa…" He touched her sleeve, his fingertips brushing along her wrist. "I need some help deciding just where I want my restaurant. Whether in a cluster of shops or a free-standing building. I have to figure out how much space I'll need…. How about you helping me with that?"

"You want me to help you?" Hands on the wheel, she stared at him.

"Yeah, sure. How about it?" His appeal

was sincere. "Maybe you even want to go in with me?"

"Not on your life. Besides, if this isn't just a pipe dream, where will you get the money to do all of this? Have you a rich uncle or something?"

"Naw, I suspect I'll have to open on a shoestring. I'll have to find used kitchen things, and stuff like that. I thought you might know where to look."

"Why would you think I would know that?"

"Well, you have a good sense of value. I think you'd be a natural at wheeling and dealing."

"Thanks for the compliment, Ethan, but I'm not sure I'd have time."

"I'm not in a rush, you know. I haven't even decided where to locate yet."

"Well, I don't have a vehicle. This is Uncle Fred's truck."

That fact settled in Ethan's mind. "We'll just have to look at places when I can take you then. How about one location at a time... on Thursdays before New Beginnings?"

She started the engine. "I'll think about it."

# Chapter Twelve

"Hi, Aunt Katherine." Lisa walked past her aunt who was holding open the door. She was feeling light and excited. Cecily came running from the kitchen.

"Hi, sweetie. How are you today?"

"Hi, Mommy." Her little arms reached out, making Lisa's heart quicken.

"Are you glad to see me?" She swept the little girl up into her own arms and nuzzled her neck. "I am sure glad to see you. You must have grown an inch since Sunday."

Cecily smelled clean and sweet, like bath powder, the kind she recalled from her own childhood. She savored these moments, which were all too few.

Her hope rose high; she was closer to her goal each day...each week. She refused to allow Aunt Katherine's threats to discourage her.

"Uh-huh. I growed two inches." The child's arms hugged Lisa's neck. Oh, Cecily felt so perfect, so soft and precious, Lisa thought, and tightened her hold.

Aunt Katherine was sober, her face set in deep lines, her eyes cold. "You can't take the child out today."

Startled, Lisa couldn't imagine what the matter was now. Hadn't Pastor Michael's visit softened her aunt even a little bit? She hadn't said, "I don't think it's a good idea," but a definite "You can't."

How dare she?

"Why not?" Lisa's heart sank. Rebelliously, she thought she could take her daughter anywhere she wanted—and keep her, for all her aunt's fussing. She'd planned to take Cecily to the park to use the swings and teeter-totter. She didn't think the child had too much fun in her life.

Aunt Katherine glanced outside, spotting Uncle Fred in the truck, waiting for them. She pursed her lips. "You can't go. I want to talk to you, Lisa."

As usual. "But—"

"In here," Aunt Katherine commanded

as she moved into the dining room. Without thought, Lisa started to follow, Cecily still in her arms.

"Not the child," Aunt Katherine stressed in no uncertain terms, then muttered under her breath, "You stupid girl—you haven't the sense God gave a goose."

"All right." Ignoring her aunt's spiteful criticism, Lisa set her child down on her feet. But it hurt to have Cecily hear such hateful words. Maybe she didn't understand them now, but she soon would, if Aunt Katherine kept up. She whispered, "Why don't you go to the front window and wave to Uncle Fred, in that truck. You haven't met him yet, but he knows all about you. See if you can get him to wave back, okay?"

She watched the little girl run to the front window, all the while fighting the need to retaliate, then slowly turned to face her aunt. "What is it?"

"I don't think you should take Cecily out."

"Why not?"

"The places you visit aren't exactly… healthy."

"What are you talking about?"

"I'm wondering what kind of mother you are."

"What kind…you know what kind of mother I am. I'm a good mother, and I'm eager to get my daughter back, you know that. Why would you say that?"

"You were seen coming out of a bar, Lisa." Aunt Katherine spoke the words with a triumphant air. She didn't make much effort to hide her pleasure at accusing Lisa. "And I won't stand for your drinking and carrying on like a—"

"Don't say it!"

Aunt Katherine's mouth pinched closed.

A flash of anger raced through Lisa as she studied her aunt. Who was Aunt Katherine to scold her as if she were still a wild teen? What right did she have?

She had to take Cecily and go, that was all there was to it. But where? Uncle Fred's miniature house? She'd been over all this before. If she were to settle there permanently, then she was afraid she would lose her ambition ever to make it on her own.

But who had seen her? Who would tattle on her? Whoever it was could make more trouble for her in the future.

Never mind that. She *had* been in a saloon for about thirty minutes, waiting for Uncle

Fred. She'd done nothing wrong. Was her aunt spying on her?

Nonsense. She shook her head slightly. What did it matter? Her aunt wasn't *that* vindictive—was she?

No more lies. Not one. I've put on the new mind of Christ, haven't I?

The words echoed in Lisa's head, but nevertheless, she felt defensive. "What of it, Aunt Katherine? I was waiting—"

"So you don't deny it?"

She lifted her chin lifted. "No, why should I? I wasn't drinking or anything. I had one cola."

Aunt Katherine made a moue, then drew her doubt out in a slow drawl. "Really?"

"I went in to see Uncle Fred, that was all. I wasn't there very long."

"Oh, Fred—" She dismissed him as though he were an insect. "I might have known. Well, that doesn't excuse it, now does it? And I don't think—"

Lisa had heard enough. Nothing would change her aunt's mind about her choices. Lisa couldn't live like a nun, however admirable that might be.

"Aunt Katherine, I am not going to stand here and argue with you. I'm wasting time."

She took a step toward the living room. Toward the front door. "Now, I planned to take Cecily out this afternoon, and I'm going to do that."

"You'd better watch your tongue, my girl, or you'll find yourself completely locked out and little Cecily with you. I can't prevent you from taking the child today, but I don't have to take any lip from you either, you know."

"Aunt Katherine—"

"That's enough." Her aunt's eyes blazed with dislike.

"I'm sorry, Aunt Katherine. I'm sorry you feel such…disapproval of my actions. But I'm going to take Cecily out this afternoon. You're welcome to come along. The park isn't far."

"No, thank you," Katherine spoke through stiff lips. "But don't be late coming back."

Lisa turned, and, walking quickly, swept Cecily up in her arms and left Aunt Katherine's house. She had to have her own place soon, no matter how small. This situation couldn't continue much longer.

But Aunt Katherine hadn't actually threatened her. She took hope in that.


"She ain't got custody, Lisa, and there's nothing to keep you from having the girl. But that's not to say the old bat won't try it on. Has she said anything more? You haven't seen any paperwork yet or nothing, have you?"

"No," Lisa mumbled, watching Cecily on a spring horse, rocking back and forth. Her curls bounced, and her tiny hands gripped the handles tightly.

Lisa was grateful her aunt hadn't pursued that line of thought.

"Well, bring the child out to my house, we'll squeeze her in."

If only they could. She yearned to say yes this instant to his idea. But where would they put a bed? In the living room? Lisa could sleep on the sofa, but who would care for Cecily while she worked? Her salary wouldn't cover day care yet.

Her aunt would really object to Uncle Fred watching Cecily. And in all honesty, Lisa didn't quite trust him not to drink too much, or fall asleep when Cecily needed him.

Lisa patted Uncle Fred on the knee, while she watched Cecily run to the sandbox. "I might, Uncle Fred. But it would turn your life upside-down."

She thought for a moment. "I've got some money saved, but it's not enough yet. If I can hold out…it'll take another two months, I figure, to have enough for an apartment. Then I can rescue…er, take Cecily out of Aunt Katherine's care."

"Why'd you leave her there in the first place, is what I'm really asking."

His old blue eyes were questioning. She gave a long sigh. Why had she?

"I was desperate to keep her out of social services, Uncle Fred." She'd been desperate, period. "No telling where she'd have ended up in the system. Aunt Katherine is hard to deal with, it's true, and she doesn't like me much, nor you, but she's trustworthy."

Uncle Fred snorted. "Yeah, she's that. You can trust 'er to make trouble, I'm thinking, and act like she's the Queen of England. But she'll take care of little Cecily for you."

Trustworthy…

Lisa thought about what that quality meant. It was true. No matter how unpleasant Aunt Katherine was, or how she sniped at Lisa, or threatened to make life miserable, she could be trusted to take care of Cecily.

*Thank you, Lord!*

Things could be worse, Lisa thought. Much worse.

Yes…thank the Lord.

She couldn't go on feeling down and out. She had her health, thank the Lord, a good enough job, and she was out of jail and free. She'd have her daughter with her just as soon as possible.

And given time, she'd know where that slimeball Rudy was hiding.

She noticed some geese on the nearby pond. "C'mon, Cecily, let's feed the geese."


"This is a possibility, Lisa." Ethan was talking about a location for his restaurant. "I just want you to have a look at it. It won't take long to decide after seeing it."

They were driving into the city. Ethan was working days this week; his shift change wasn't permanent, but it gave them the same time at work. And the same free time, too, which seemed to please him no end, Lisa thought.

"But I have three others to visit, too."

"I don't think we'll have time to see a whole bunch of sites, Ethan." She wanted to get to the library before it closed, and it was late afternoon now. But no way would she tell Ethan that. She didn't want him to know about her network search for Rudy.

She glanced at him, wondering what his argument would be for persuading her to go with him. He surprised her by giving her a narrow-eyed stare, then grinning. "Okay."

Her answer was a return smile.

They pulled up in front of an empty shop at the end of a line of brick storefronts. The neighborhood had seen better days. Instantly, she felt negative about the site.

"Uh…" mumbled Ethan, his gaze flying everywhere. The five other stores were all occupied, but were rundown. "Well, let's look at it anyway."

"It's too small," Lisa muttered as they got out of the car. She put her hands around her eyes and pressed her face to the dirty window. "You'd never have enough space for tables *and* your band."

"Uh-uh, I guess not," he agreed. "No wonder the rent is so low. Okay, let's go." He opened the car door for her, then leaned down to brush dirt from her nose. He swiftly bent to place a kiss there, half smiling, then went around to his side of the car.

"What was that for?" Lisa rubbed her nose, gazing at him suspiciously.

"Just keeping my companion clean." He flicked a glance her way, a half grin telling her nothing. "It's something I've grown used to doing with my kids."

"I'm not one of your kids, you know."

"Nope." He started the car once more. "Believe me, I wasn't thinking of you that way."

"Well, don't." She buckled her seat belt. "I'm a parent myself."

Uh-huh. Ethan wondered when he would meet her little girl. He wondered about a lot of things where Lisa was concerned.

"Well, we have time to look at the next place, don't we?" he asked.

"Sure, if it's not too far."

It took only moments to travel the few miles to the next site on his list. They pulled up to the curb a block and a half from the property, parking being a problem. They got out and strolled down the street. A hair salon and nail place occupied the corner. Then an empty store. Then an antiques and used furniture shop. By the time they reached the site listed, Ethan was shaking his head.

"There's a lot of cars around, and the neighborhood is healthier, but I don't think so. Let's go."

When they returned to the car, Lisa glanced over his shoulder while he looked at his list.

"What about that place by Independence Square?" Lisa asked. "What would be wrong with that location?"

"Haven't looked at it. Can you go now?"

"If we hurry."

It took them thirty minutes to reach the place. Located on a side street just off the square, the site sat empty, bordered by another empty storefront and a dusty used-book store. When someone peeked out the window of the bookstore and waved, Ethan felt warmed.

"This place has possibilities…"

The property had been a hardware store in its former existence. And it had a balcony.

Ethan rubbed a circle on the glass, and looked through. Lisa did the same.

"There are floorboards missing in that corner," she said.

"Uh-huh. Wonder what caused that. And what's in those boxes?" He referred to a stack of cardboard boxes against the wall.

They turned away to inspect the neighborhood. "There's a parking lot at the bottom of the street," Ethan exclaimed.

"Yeah, but there's not much traffic."

"There could be. If we pour money into advertising."

"Well, yes. But that costs a fortune."

"It might be worth it." He stood gazing around at the half-empty buildings. "Okay, this is definitely a possibility."

"Let's go see the fourth site on your list," she said eagerly.

"What about your time limit?"

"Oh, um, I was only going to the library. I guess it can wait."

He chuckled and grabbed her hand, lifting it and kissing the knuckles. "Aren't you glad you came?"

Lisa sat at the library computer, searching the few chat sites she knew Rudy frequented. At least he had before his flight. Most were sites for singles and some were erotic. He hadn't known she knew of them—but she'd found them one day when she'd gone searching for information concerning a client for the firm.

By that point she'd become suspicious of his activities. She'd caught him in too many lies. But by the time her suspicions had proven true and she was about to confront him, the law had intruded, and Rudy had disappeared. Leaving her holding the incriminating papers…papers she'd signed for Rudy.

She was certain he'd show up on one of these sites sometime; he was fascinated by the women he could meet on the Internet. After two years, he would feel safe.

He could use a fake name, but she trusted herself to know his speech patterns, his come-on lines.

And tonight she thought she'd found something.

The library flashed its lights, and she sighed. She closed the computer with reluctance and left to walk the four blocks to catch Uncle Fred at Benny's Pub. She hoped leaving his buddies early didn't bother him too much.

She tucked her jacket up about her ears. A cold front had come through, and her face felt it. She hurriedly made her way along the neighborhood streets, admiring the colorful Christmas lights on the houses.

What did Cecily want for Christmas?

She saw the strip mall ahead. It was after nine, and the stores were closed. The only lights were from the corner saloon. Benny's had a reasonable crowd tonight, she thought.

Then she slowed. A police car sat in the parking lot. She spotted one man behind the wheel. Was he the only officer there? Had something happened at the bar?

She couldn't go in….

Turning, she walked swiftly away, past the convenience store, past the cleaners, and down the side street. She'd get home another way. She could walk the distance.

A vehicle drove up slowly behind her. She looked over her shoulder, immediately recognizing Uncle Fred's truck. He stopped, and she ran to get in.

"Uncle Fred! Boy, am I ever glad to see you."

"I was looking for you, girl."

"I saw the police, and I just couldn't…I shouldn't be there."

"I understand."

"Why were they there?"

"Don't know. They been hanging around for maybe half an hour." Uncle Fred glanced at her as he turned a corner. "But they were looking for somebody. Maybe you."

"Me?" Her brows shot up. "But why? I've only been there once in my life, and I… Aunt Katherine? Do you think she'd stoop so low?"

"Doesn't matter what I think."

It was something Aunt Katherine would do, all right.

"Well, I won't try that again. I'll just have

to walk home from the library, since I don't want to spend the taxi money."

"Naw, don't do that, Lisa. It's a bit of a hike after a long day on your feet. I'll come along and pick you up. What time does the library close?"

The offer surprised her. "Nine. You'd do that?"

"No other way, is there? I'd do it and a lot more to foil that old bat. She's had her fun with the baby long enough. You gotta get Cecily back. Sooner you get your apartment, the better, I'm thinking."

Uncle Fred knew of her struggles. He understood her torn heart over not having Cecily with her.

"Oh, Uncle Fred. I love you...."

"Why, honey...I never doubted that. But it's nice to hear it. I love you, too. I'm only sorry I wasn't there when you had your trouble."

Sudden tears formed, and she sniffed. Uncle Fred had lived much of his life in Cleveland. If he'd been around when she was growing up, would her life have turned out differently? She hadn't known the Lord then.

All at once, she could see Aunt Katherine's point of view. Lisa had been extremely rebellious in her teen years, and her twenties hadn't been much better. Only in her thirties had she tried to change her life. She'd tried to make her life meaningful.

Her tentative faith sustained her now. With God's help, she *would* change her life. No matter how difficult that was. Cecily deserved a mother who had it all together. She deserves a better life, too.

"Me, too," she murmured softly. "But you've done me a big favor tonight, Uncle Fred, and I'm very grateful."

"'Nuff said. Now what's your plans?"

# Chapter Thirteen

The wind blew sharply and Lisa hugged her coat close about her chin as she entered Aunt Katherine's house on Christmas Eve. She'd called yesterday to say she was taking Cecily for the holiday, but still, she knew she'd have a fight on her hands. But she was going to be with Cecily for Christmas, and that was that.

The thought of celebrating her first Christmas as a Christian awed her. Just last night, the words of the carol "O Holy Night" had had her in tears. She'd heard the words a dozen times through, for more than three times a dozen Christmases, yet she'd never listened with such attentiveness as this year. Now she believed all those Christmas songs; she believed what they had to say about

Christ. But still, she wanted everything just right…for her daughter and herself. And that was going to take a fight.

Surprisingly, Uncle Mark supported her decision about taking Cecily with her. Aunt Katherine stood tight-lipped having accepted Lisa's small gift, a small glass dish she was sure her aunt would like, while Lisa got Cecily ready to leave.

The minute they were out the door, Lisa felt lighter. She wanted to shout her happiness. She couldn't keep the grin from spreading across her face as she led her little girl down the steps and into the old truck where Uncle Fred waited patiently. This was a test in a way. In a big way. She wanted to see how Cecily could fit into Uncle Fred's tiny space.

The evening was pleasant enough, but the night was miserable. Cecily, in her mother's bed, cried until Lisa lay down with her. But the bed was too narrow for them both. Once Cecily fell asleep, Lisa went out to the lumpy old sofa, which she had made up with blankets. It was uncomfortable to sleep on, and she was awake a good part of the night.

Lisa consoled herself with the promise of the next day. They'd been invited to Christmas dinner at Ethan's house.

They drove into the middle-class neighborhood about noon on Christmas Day, and looked for the correct address. The street was full of brick houses, all with fireplaces and triple-car garages. Lisa bit her lip. Ethan called this modest?

It was a far cry from Uncle Fred's tiny rundown house. A wave of shame and embarrassment crawled over her. From somewhere deep inside, she felt the old emotions—lack of self-worth and helplessness. She had nothing.

Never mind. She had Cecily and Uncle Fred.

Ethan met them at the door with a mug of hot cider to welcome them, and a smile as bright as his Christmas tree. The house smelled of ham and sweet potatoes, and the children greeted each other with glee.

The day was perfect. They watched old movies after dinner, funny ones that made them all laugh, then played with Ethan's children's new train set beside the Christmas tree. Lisa and Ethan talked in snatches about the progress of Ethan's restaurant, which was now on its way to become a reality.

When it was finally time to go home, they all said goodbyes, and Lisa, Uncle Fred and

Cecily headed out to the truck. Uncle Fred pulled a bottle from his coat pocket, the whiskey smell strong inside the truck's cab. He took a deep pull and muttered, "That's better."

Lisa said nothing. After all, it was Uncle Fred's life. It didn't take away from his kindness or loving ability. She only hoped he hadn't had enough to affect his driving.

She glanced down at her daughter. Cecily had fallen asleep already, cuddled next to her on the seat.

When Lisa carried a tired Cecily in to Aunt Katherine's house, a small depression enveloped her. She'd have to stick to her original plans. Wait until she could afford a place of her own. As loving as he was, Uncle Fred drank too much. There was no way she'd bring Cecily into such an environment.

Ethan planned to open his restaurant in February, he hoped by Valentine's Day. But he was beginning to doubt he could pull it together by then. If he couldn't, he hoped for March. He'd attract customers with a spring-fling theme.

Regardless, he and Lisa had worked hard during their free time. Only last week, he'd purchased the latest in kitchen equipment—with Lisa's input. Surprisingly, they'd been able to accomplish quite a lot during the Christmas holidays.

He thought of the recent holidays. He'd enjoyed them more this year, taking pleasure in making them bright and happy for his kids. And Christmas Day had definitely been fun.

He'd joined the activities at New Beginnings with gusto. And he took the spiritual teachings he'd learned and put them to work in his own life. He thought of the recent scripture from Romans that they'd covered in Bible Study:

*Who shall separate us from the love of Christ? Shall trouble or hardship or persecution or famine or nakedness or danger or sword?*

*As it is written, For Your sake we face death all day long; we are considered as sheep to be slaughtered."*

*No, in all these things we are more than conquerors through Him who loved us. For I am convinced that neither death nor life, neither angels nor demons, nor anything else in all crea-*

*tion, will be able to separate us from the love of God that is in Christ Jesus our Lord.*

That scripture comforted him. He felt it deep in his soul. Christ Jesus, always with him? He marveled at that, and tried to wrap his mind around the truth.

Surprisingly, he'd been able to let go of Sharon's death more easily lately. There would always be a place for her in his heart, but somehow, her passing didn't tear at him the way it had before. Ready to move on, he felt more than a little excitement about his restaurant. It made him feel like a kid again. Life seemed full of promise...

"I hope I'm not fooling myself." He murmured the rare doubt aloud as he parked his car in front of the building space he'd leased for his new business. "But if I am, I'm enjoying the stuffing out of the experience."

Lisa had been there before him, he knew. Before she'd gone to work. The woman was a godsend. She knew more about getting crews to work on time than he thought possible. How did she do it?

And Lisa was often with him these days. She and little Cecily and Uncle Fred had joined him and his kids on Christmas Day for dinner, and wonder of wonders, all the kids had played happily. He and Lisa had simply sat and watched them, enjoying their coffee in peace.

Before Lisa had left at the end of the evening, Ethan had pulled her into the kitchen and kissed her a tender good-night. The kiss was not as long as he'd have liked, and not as thorough, but the exchange gave him hope.

*Tender* was the word…her lips felt softer than velvet…and her warm response sent waves of hope racing up his spine.

He felt restless as he climbed out of the car now. He hadn't felt this level of hope for a long time.

Only, his progress with her was so slow! It frustrated the daylights out of him. He tried to show her affection by word and deed… when she allowed it. In return she put him off and didn't let him get close, talking about the progress on the restaurant instead of personal matters. If she wasn't so uncommunicative.

Something troubled her. He was beginning to know her well enough now to see that. He was waiting to hear her complete story—and not very patiently, he admitted only to himself. But with the new patience he had developed.

But she was no less a godsend, he thought as he got out of the car. She'd focused on his restaurant as if it were a lodestar, and his plans had shot forward like a rocket this last month. She visited the location and kept after his workmen each day with composure and a knowledge of what was to be done. Obviously, she was used to taking charge, and doing it well. He wondered about that.

As he entered the site now, he shivered with the January cold. Time to turn on the heat, he guessed. Then he noticed a couple of men putting in a new back door. A blast of cold air blew through.

"Hi, guys. Mmm…the door looks good."

"Fine," said the big man hanging it. "We'll be done here in a little while."

"Great." That meant he could now lock the place at night. He glanced around, trying to see if anything else from his list had been done.

After a brief inspection, he left, driving straight to work. His babysitter and after-school care were new…again. Guided by Michael at New Beginnings, he'd hired an older woman, and he hoped she'd last until spring.

He strode into the Blue Bird Café with thoughts swirling, ready for work. He'd graduated to the grill as a short-order cook. The more complicated entrées were still prepared by the head cook, but Ethan observed the food preparation carefully, filing away facts in his mind for future use. He knew he could do this in his own restaurant until he could hire a chef.

Voices, louder than usual, snapped him out of his thoughts. He stopped, glancing over at the three people standing near the kitchen exit into the public area. Lisa…

Her mouth drooped slightly, and there were creases between her eyebrows. Something had made her unhappy.

In fact, he thought he'd never seen her with the look of anger mixed with sadness that appeared in her eyes now. He wondered what was going on.

Another waitress, Marie, who had been employed at the restaurant longest, talked rapidly with Mac, the manager.

"Now, Marie, just settle down," said Mac. "Keep your voice down, you're making the customers nervous. You don't know that Lisa, here, took your money."

"She did, I'm sure she did." The accusation stood out like a flashing red stoplight.

"I didn't!" exclaimed Lisa. Her mouth closed tightly, almost in desperation.

He started around the little group toward her.

"She's lying," exclaimed the other waitress, her brown eyes snapping, hands on her hips. "She was a long time combing her hair, I'm thinking. She could've easily gone through my pockets in the time she was back there."

"I'm not lying!" Lisa's back was pressed against the door frame. She looked pale. Ethan thought if she attempted to move away from the support right now she'd fall down. "Why do you think I am? What have I done for you to accuse me so?"

Several employees gathered around the group, creating a barrier between him and Lisa. He stopped.

Mac tried to wave them away. "Get along, you folks. Back to your jobs. Take care of the customers."

They scattered away, but remained close—within hearing. Ethan stayed where he was.

Marie tossed her head, accusation leaping from her gaze. There wasn't an ounce of softness there, and no forgiveness at all. She wanted blood. "That money was there in my coin purse, in my coat pocket! Nearly fifteen dollars. It's little enough, but I should've put it away, knowing what I know about you."

What did she know?

"What do you mean?" asked Lisa.

"I mean you…you've been to jail. People who've stolen money once…" Less certain now, Marie lowered her voice.

Lisa's hand spread across her stomach, as if she'd sustained a belly punch. She bit her lip and a haunted look entered her eyes. Her voice dropped to a near whisper. "But I didn't take your money!"

"You were the only one in the locker room," said Marie. "And we've been losing tip money ever since you came to work here."

"Now wait a minute, girls—" The manager tried to intervene. He turned to Lisa. "I'm not saying you took the money or anything like that, Lisa, but…with your background… I mean, it wouldn't hurt to let us search your stuff, now would it? Is your purse in your locker?"

Lisa gasped. "Search my—? How dare you! I've told you I didn't take it."

"I won't touch anything," Mac insisted.

"I just want you to empty your purse yourself so we can see if—if—uh—"

"But anyone could've slipped into the back room and gone through the coat pockets. Sherry, maybe," Lisa muttered in desperation, "or Sammy or John. Even Steve from the evening shift was hanging about this morning when I arrived. What about him?"

"See? She's trying to divert suspicion elsewhere. I'm not going to put up with it anymore," declared the other woman defiantly. "I lost some tips last week, right off the tables. I bet she took 'em. I didn't say anything 'cause I wasn't sure. But if she doesn't give that money back now, I'm going to call the police."

Lisa looked at her shoes for half a second, then raised her chin and straightened her spine. She marched over to the lockers and, taking out her purse, emptied the contents onto the chair there. Ethan spotted tears in her eyes, but he knew Lisa. She was red-hot fighting mad now…

Her black billfold lay there, a couple of tissues on top. Pens and sunglasses. Her comb and small makeup mirror tumbled to the side, her keys clanking to the floor.

"Check the change purse, Mac. Go ahead, it's okay. I have two quarters, a dime and three pennies."

The manager backed up a step and shook his head. "Not me, Lisa."

"You, Marie? Do you want to see how much money I have? I have ten dollars beside the change. It's not enough to buy much, but it's all I have."

Marie merely flashed her a sour gaze.

"So call the police," Lisa continued. "I don't care."

"Now, now, girls…um, don't be that way," said Mac. "We don't need the police, do we?"

Mac knew the presence of the police would create negative publicity for the restaurant. He didn't want them here.

The flash in Lisa's eyes told Ethan that Mac had said the wrong thing. Lisa wasn't a girl, and she wouldn't appreciate his condescending, patronizing approach.

"Well, I won't work with her," declared Marie. "Either she goes or I do."

"Now, Marie, be reasonable…" said Mac, turning as he spotted two customers leave without being seated. Others were craning their necks to see what was going on.

"That's okay, Mac. I'm going. I wouldn't work here any longer when I'm accused of stealing. I quit." Lisa threw down her apron and shoved the scattered items into her purse. Mac and Marie left her alone, but Ethan stayed, leaning against the locker next to hers.

"Lisa, sweetheart, I'm sorry. What started all this, anyway? What was it all about?"

"I don't really know, but I'm outta here." She pushed past him with lightning speed, her pale face mutinous.

Outside, she stopped abruptly. Ethan followed.

"What is it? What's wrong?"

"Uncle Fred dropped me off this morning. He wanted to use the truck today."

"Oh. Well, come on, I'll take you home."

"I should call a cab," she said tentatively, trying to hide her misery. "You shouldn't be troubled."

"Nonsense. All the work you're doing for me, I should provide you with a car. Why haven't I thought of that?" An idea came to him. "And I know just where I can find one, too."

His sister had an older car she was trying to sell. It would need some repair, but it was in pretty good condition. In fact, he could probably find someone to fix it from the New Beginnings bunch.

She looked at him skeptically. "What about your position here? You can't leave... you've got to go to work."

She was right. He wanted to work at least another month.

"Look, you take my car." He quickly dug out his keys and handed them over. As he closed her fingers over them, he noted the strain in her face. He softened his voice. "You can pick me up later, when I get off work."

"Are you sure?" Accepting the keys, she gave him a doubtful gaze.

"Sure, I'm sure. You can check on those painters who are supposed to be working at the site today. In fact, you'll be doing me a favor by overseeing everything. I couldn't be there to meet with the foreman, so I'd appreciate if you'd check with him. Here's his name..."

"Are you comin' to work or do I wipe your name from the roster, too?" shouted Mac from the back door.

"I'll be right there." Ethan turned back to Lisa, pulling out a slip of paper from his pocket. There was more to the stolen money incident, but now wasn't the time to upset Lisa by asking questions. "Don't worry. Waitress jobs are easy to get, and you can work for me if you want to. We'll get by…"

Lisa took a deep breath. "All right. I'll go there directly…and I'll pick you up at the close of your shift here. Thanks, Ethan."

Lisa got into Ethan's car and turned on the heater. Its warm blast reminded her how uncomfortable the old truck was becoming. Poor Uncle Fred.

Poor me, she thought, as overwhelming emotion threatened to rob her of the recent peace she'd been struggling to find. She'd been out of jail almost four months, and she was no better off now than she was then. No job, no apartment, no car.

She put her forehead down on the wheel and let the tears come. She cried for ten minutes. *I've got to do something… Lord, why aren't You here?*

Then came the thought… It isn't true that I have nothing…I have a place to live with Uncle Fred…and almost enough money for the tiniest apartment, the down payment and all… I'll have saved enough soon…and by letting Aunt Katherine keep Cecily, I've kept her out of foster care. That's a plus. Aunt Katherine is creating difficulties, it's true, but I'd have it even harder if Cecily were in foster care.

And I have Jesus…

But she'd been accused of stealing once again. That was undeserved. She'd paid back as much as she could to the company. Hearing Marie's accusation was horrible. And how could she have found out about Lisa's background? What did she know?

But Lisa hadn't taken anything from Marie, nor had she rifled through the coats in the employees' locker room. If tips were missing, someone else had taken them. In time, she hoped, they'd discover that it wasn't her.

That didn't do her any good now. Frustrated at her weakness, she found a tissue in her purse and wiped her eyes and blew her nose. Crying wouldn't solve anything. She sat up straighter and looked out at the parking lot.

Time to leave. She was a tough cookie, she reminded herself.

Starting the car, she decided that she'd spend some of her day at the library, by golly. Looking for Rudy was the best antidote she knew for the blues. She'd find that low-bellied skunk yet, and then she'd…

A vision of Rudy, hanging helplessly by his heels, flailing uselessly, made her blood pressure rise with excitement. It would serve the rat right, and she'd dance to celebrate.

*Vengeance is mine, saith the Lord…*

She could hear Beth Anne's voice, a memory of a Bible Study she'd done in jail. It niggled at the edges of Lisa's consciousness…

But how could she just let it all go? Surely the Lord wouldn't hold her to account for wanting to catch Rudy and bring him to justice.

She wouldn't be satisfied until she did. And she was close to finding him.

Her mouth firmed. Never mind the Caribbean. There was a Web site in Mexico… she'd found something on the Net that sounded just too much like Rudy. She'd been itching to investigate further.

## Chapter Fourteen

As soon as she entered the main library, the tears barely wiped from her eyes, Lisa headed straight to the computers. They were all in use. Holding her frustration in check, she swung on her heel and went to the library desk.

"When will the next computer be free?"

"Oh, let's see…" the young clerk's blond hair swung about her face as she glanced at the clock. "Two will be free in about ten minutes or so."

"Oh, that's not long," Lisa answered, feeling relief. She'd just stew about the fight at the restaurant if she had too long to wait.

Once she'd given her name to reserve a computer, Lisa sat down near the desks. She picked up a magazine, flipping through at a rapid pace. She was determined to get her mind off the hateful expression Marie had worn when she'd accused Lisa of stealing.

Lisa stared at an ad listed in the magazine. Jobs were easy enough to find. She'd have another before the week was out.

But she wondered, how had Marie known about Lisa's background? How had she known Lisa had served time for stealing? It didn't matter that she'd been caught up in Rudy's greater scheme of embezzlement, or that she'd suffered the consequences just as if she'd been totally guilty. Or that she'd been somewhat a victim herself.

Oh, it was all so confused.

She was old enough to know better, Lisa chastised herself. She'd been more than merely naive about Rudy. She'd been stupid, stupid, stupid to sign the papers that had ticked off the whole scheme. And she was paying the price.

Pulling in a deep breath, she then let it out slowly. She took another, and another.

Obviously, Marie had wanted to get Lisa fired. And in an ugly, hurtful way…with a public scene.

But how had the woman found out? And to accuse her in front of her boss?

Had Aunt Katherine…? Oh, no…no.

But the doubt wouldn't go away, and Lisa remembered the time Aunt Katherine had finagled a way to make a woman she disliked leave her own church. That was old news, but it did put Aunt Katherine in a somewhat suspicious light.

Oh, surely she wouldn't go so far to get Lisa fired…would she? She couldn't be so devious!

Lisa stared out over the book racks with unseeing eyes. Suddenly she rose, the magazine slipping from her lap. She hurried to the front desk.

"Um, I'm sorry," she told the blond clerk. "I've got to leave. Can…can you reserve a computer for me at—" she glanced at the clock "—at this time tomorrow?"

"Sure," replied the woman. "Your name again?"

But Lisa was already on her way out.

Aunt Katherine knew how to get to her. Stealing tips! As though she'd stoop to such petty thievery, she mused as she hurriedly climbed into the car.

Though the accusation caused Lisa a great deal of pain, she couldn't let that make her do anything foolish. It would be too easy to get her sent back to jail.

And too easy for Aunt Katherine to gain complete custody of Cecily. Not that she'd ever sign her own rights away, Lisa thought.

As she put the key into the ignition, she paused. Aunt Katherine would never admit to bribing Marie—she wouldn't even admit she knew her. But as sure as she was sitting in the library parking lot, Lisa was convinced of Aunt Katherine's meddling. And Cecily was in her care.

Her real and present enemy was Aunt Katherine! Lisa realized. She had to think of a way to win her over. But would it be before Aunt Katherine utterly ruined Lisa? Broke her spirit down? Destroyed her chance to raise her child in peace?

*Lord, my reputation is already ruined. I'm trying to rebuild it. I don't need Aunt Katherine working against me.*

But the damage had been done before Lisa knew the Lord Jesus.

*I am not the same person as before. Didn't that count for anything? Didn't He promise that all things would be made new? Didn't He promise never to leave her…or forsake her?*

*Well, if that's true, Lord Jesus, I need You now. Please…help me…*

She glanced at her watch. Determinedly, she started Ethan's car. In the back of her mind, she appreciated the fact that he had let her use it, and that it ran smoothly.

When she reached her aunt's house, she hurried up the stairs and impatiently rang the bell. Nothing. She listened for movement inside, but silence greeted her.

Blast it, there was no one home.

Lisa turned, wondering what she should do. Wait for her aunt to return home with Cecily? That could take hours. If she only knew where they'd gone. But she didn't. She'd have to come back.

Ethan had asked her to go to the restaurant site. She'd take care of that now.

She found the painters hard at work and glanced at their progress with thankfulness. At least something was going right. The walls held a first coat of paint, a soft buttery beige.

"Where are the accent tiles?" she asked Barney, the crew chief, as she checked the boxes that had arrived during the morning.

"Haven't seen them."

"They should be here. The tile guy is going to be working tomorrow." She borrowed the mobile phone to make a call to the supplier.

For the rest of the afternoon she worked alongside the men, overseeing the installation of the counters. It was after six when she left. She headed back toward the library on the chance a computer was available. But all of them were in use, and she left in mild annoyance.

She drove back to Aunt Katherine's house. Her aunt and uncle were home, and had just finished dinner.

"What are you doing here?" Aunt Katherine gave her usual sour stare.

Couldn't her aunt ask anything new? Katherine stood blocking the doorway. From the back of the kitchen, she heard Cecily chattering.

"I've come to see Cecily, Aunt Katherine." Lisa kept her tone even, but determined. "But besides that, I have something I want to talk to you about."

"I don't think so, not now. I'm tired, and I plan to have an early night." She moved to shut the storm door and the door frame. "And I've let you see Cecily too much, to my way of thinking. She's getting spoiled."

Lisa's hands balled into fists. She'd had this argument too many times, groveled too much to make good sense. It was time she took the situation into her own hands. Never mind that she'd have to make do at Uncle Fred's tiny house. A couple of months, that was all.

"She's my child, Aunt Katherine," she said as she held the door open. "You have no right to keep me from her."

Her aunt stood solidly before Lisa. "That may be, but I have rights myself. And I don't want you here just now. I have my resources."

Lisa stepped back and stared. Her aunt wasn't going to let her into the house!

She tipped her head, studying the face in front of her. Aunt Katherine suddenly looked old. Deep lines bracketed deeply around her mouth, and the skin sagged under her eyes and chin. The woman *was* old, Lisa thought with some pity. Did that account for her fight to keep Cecily? Did she fear growing older?

Compassion came down on Lisa like a warm shower. But it only strengthened her resolve to get her daughter back. She couldn't waste a single day of Cecily's growing up.

"You have your plans, too, don't you, Aunt Katherine?" she said more softly, allowing her pity to surface. "Do you know I got fired from my job today?"

A victorious light suddenly flared in the old woman's eyes. "No, I didn't know that. My, my. Old habits catch up with you, did they?"

"What do you mean by that?"

"I mean I'm only surprised the job lasted as long as it did." She looked down her nose at Lisa. "You couldn't expect them to keep you after the management found out about your past, could you?"

"The management knew, Aunt Katherine. I didn't lie when I made out my application. You don't know anything about it. Or do you?"

Her aunt raised her chin, but didn't reply. Her blue eyes were hard and unyielding.

Cecily's voice sounded louder, as though the little girl were coming to see who was at the door.

Lisa said more quickly, "But that's not the problem now. I want my daughter…my Cecily…and I want her now."

For the first time, she saw fear in Aunt Katherine's eyes. Her hand tightened on the door handle.

"You can't see her now, Lisa. I'll be putting the child to bed right away. She'll get all excited if she sees you and won't be able to sleep."

But Lisa had had enough. She shoved gently but firmly past her aunt.

"Here, here…if you…here, you can't… I'll call the police." Her aunt's hands flailed as she tried to grab Lisa's arm to stop her.

Lisa stopped, just inside the door, and looked at her. "Do that, Aunt Katherine. Just try to stop me."

Then she turned and stared at Uncle Mark. He gave a slight nod, his expression knowing, and smiled gently.

Lisa's heart lifted. No matter the problems she would face, she was doing the right thing.

Then her daughter hit her legs, hugging tightly. "Mommy!"

"Hi, sweetheart." She leaned down to lift the child and return the hug. "How are you?"

"Fine. I don't want to go to bed. It's too early, right?"

"Right." Lisa brushed aside the hair that had fallen in Cecily's eyes. "How would you like to come with me tonight?"

"Okay. Can we see Endure?"

"Yep…that's exactly what we'll do."

"And Uncle Fred?"

"Uh-huh. Uncle Fred, too."

"Now, Lisa…you can't take her out so late…" Her aunt's voice was high-pitched.

"Let's pack your things," Lisa said, ignoring Aunt Katherine. She had her arms tightly around her daughter as she walked into the little room.

"If you go now, you can never come back. Never."

Lisa didn't reply. She'd heard the threats too many times.

"You don't believe me?" Her aunt's voice rose even higher.

Setting Cecily down, Lisa grabbed a pillow case and started stuffing her daughter's clothes into it. Shoes, underthings. She ignored the dresses in the closet. She hurriedly glanced about for Cecily's coat. Uncle Mark handed it to her as Lisa heard her aunt dial the phone.

"I'm calling your parole officer," her aunt stated.

"Fine. I'll call her, too. She's an understanding woman. But I don't think you'll find her in the office now."

She lifted Cecily into her arms once more and left the house. She had noted earlier that Jordan's car seat was still buckled in the back, and she placed Cecily there.

She drove straight to Uncle Fred's place. He was out, as she'd expected. While Cecily greeted the dog, Lisa placed the bag of clothes in the bedroom, then sagged onto the couch. She'd done it now. But having her child with her would be worth everything.

When it was almost time to put Cecily to bed, Lisa rummaged through the clothes she'd brought. Oh, swell. She'd forgotten the child's socks…and pajamas. What else?

Well, she wasn't going back to Aunt Katherine's, that was for sure. She pulled out her small notebook and found the emergency number for her parole officer. Might as well tell her what had happened before Aunt Katherine made a stink.

"Mommy, can Endure sleep with me?"

"She usually sleeps with Uncle Fred, but I suppose this once…"

"Yaay!"

Mrs. Braddock picked up the phone, and Lisa launched into her news.

"I don't see why not, Lisa. You'll work harder knowing your child depends on you. Now where are you thinking of looking for work?"

Lisa mentioned a couple of places.

"That's fine, dear. Just report to me as soon as you secure a new job. When is your usual time to come in?"

"Another couple of weeks."

"Good. I'll make a note of this call, and we'll be set straight. Good-night, Lisa."

A weight rolled off Lisa's shoulders. Keeping right with the courts was all-important now. She thought of calling Beth Anne, but Cecily needed attention.

"C'mon, honey, how about getting ready for bed? You'll have to sleep in a T-shirt of mine for the night. I forgot your pajamas."

Cecily giggled. "Okay. Tomorrow is school. Can you take me?"

"Sure enough, sweetie pie," Lisa said as she fingered Cecily's curls. "We're going to do lots of things together from now on. I promise you that."

Lisa put Cecily to bed, spending time telling her stories and singing her songs. Finally, the child fell asleep.

She began to worry Uncle Fred would be late coming home. She called Benny's, the pub he frequented, but the bartender said he wasn't there. As she hung up the phone, she bit her lip, thinking, *Now what do I do?* She had to return Ethan's car.

Uncle Fred came home at ten o'clock. "Whose car is that in the driveway?"

"Ethan's."

He glanced about the room. "Where is he?"

"At work, I presume," she said, grabbing her coat.

"Have you been home all this time? I went to pick you up, and they told me—"

"I know, I know. I was fired today...or rather I quit." Lisa made a beeline toward the front door, shoving her arm through the sleeve of her coat. She softened her tone. "I borrowed the car, so now I have to go and pick him up. He'll be looking for me... And I went by and picked up Cecily, Uncle Fred. She's asleep in the bedroom."

"You did?" His face lit up with a smile. "Well, well...for permanent?"

"Yep. For permanent." She tried to keep her weariness from showing.

"I like that. Like it a lot. I'd like to of seen your aunt's face. Imagine she was put out some." He grinned.

Hearing voices, the dog came out of the bedroom. She jumped up on Fred to be greeted.

"You could say that. Now, Uncle Fred,

you haven't had so much to drink that you'll…I mean, you won't fall asleep while I'm gone, will you? I need you to stay alert for Cecily."

"Nah…I'm good, Lisa girl. I've been doing better since you've been here, y'know. Don't drink as much."

"I did know that, Uncle Fred." She kissed him on the cheek, smelling the beer on his breath. Nevertheless, she offered him praise. "And it pleases me to the nth degree that you're more sober these days. Now I'm late for picking up Ethan. I have to run. But we'll talk about it in the morning, okay?"

She was out the door even as Uncle Fred said, "All right."

Ethan had finished work fifteen minutes ago, and it would take Lisa twenty minutes to get there. Too bad she didn't have a cell phone.

She risked five miles over the speed limit. Surely she wouldn't get stopped for that.

The restaurant lot was almost empty when she pulled up in front of the figure leaning against the employees' door. She left the motor running and scooted over to the passenger seat.

"Where have you been?" Ethan asked,

flashing her an annoyed glance as he climbed into the driver's side and buckled his seat belt. "You're thirty minutes late."

"Sorry, Ethan. It couldn't be helped. I—"

"Thirty minutes, mind you. Not five."

"Yes, and I'm sorry. Take a right at the next corner."

"Not even a phone call." He turned where she directed, then asked, "Where have you been all this time?"

"I went by the restaurant site as you asked me to do, and I got caught up in the work. I had to call the store to find out where the accent tiles were, then I checked the counters…."

"Okay, okay. You were busy all afternoon, I take it." His tone was still angry. "But that didn't take all your attention, did it?"

"Yes it did! I was there until six o'clock."

"All right, then." He seemed somewhat mollified. "But where were you afterward?"

"You need to turn left at the next light."

"Okay." Ethan frowned slightly. The neighborhood wasn't the best, he noted. It was rundown, and a lot of the small houses needed repair. Trash littered the street. "So?"

"I went to get my daughter."

"Cecily?" He glanced at her. Something

was really wrong. He let go of his anger, noticing her troubled expression. Was she that hurt over getting fired? Or had something else happened? "She's with you? I didn't think you were scheduled to see her till Saturday?"

"No, I wasn't. But I've had it with Aunt Katherine. It's just too much. She thinks she can manipulate me into letting go of my rights with my own daughter. The very idea! And the longer I leave Cecily with her, the meaner Aunt Katherine becomes. She just…I can't prove it, but I know she did something to make it seem…to cause Marie to accuse me of stealing that money…I just wish I knew how."

"But that's ludicrous!" he said, flashing her a glance. "How could your aunt do anything?"

He noticed how tightly her hands were clasped; he thought her control was tenuous at best. What was going on here? "She wouldn't know anyone at the Blue Bird Café!"

Lisa ignored his observation, merely saying, "Pull up in that gravel drive. This is Uncle Fred's house."

"This is it?"

"Yeah, this one."

It looked as though a bulldozer wouldn't go amiss. Lisa hadn't said much about her uncle's place—she'd mentioned it was tiny, but sheesh.... Built around the 1920s, the house—the whole neighborhood—had seen better days.

Ignoring his reaction, Lisa continued talking. "It sounds paranoid, I know, to suspect Aunt Katherine of—of spying, and trying to—to pull something so underhanded. But I—"

"Lisa, what's going on?" Ethan asked as he pushed the brake pedal and turned off the motor. "I want to know."

"Yes, well...I have to go in now. Cecily will be waiting."

"Is she still awake at this hour?"

"No. She's asleep."

"Is Uncle Fred waiting up?"

She glanced at the one lighted window. "Um, probably not, but I'd better go in anyway and check if he...um, left anything on or...something. But what about you? Don't you have to get home? Your babysitter—"

"She's staying the night. Come on, honey, spill it."

# *Chapter Fifteen*

Lisa glanced at the silent house. Uncle Fred would be nodding in front of the television. It wasn't fair to keep him from his bed.

She sighed deeply and brushed her hair behind her ear. "Your children are okay?"

"Yeah, for tonight anyway. Georgie Dene is filling in for the regular sitter, but she has to leave early in the morning. Now, how about it, Lisa? Are you going to tell me what's going on?"

"Okay." She pushed down the door handle. She'd put this off long enough. The truth couldn't be much worse than what he imagined. What anyone in New Beginnings imagined, she thought. "Come on in, I suppose. Then Uncle Fred can go to bed."

They were quiet when they entered the house.

"Hi, Uncle Fred," Lisa said. "Thanks for waiting up for me. Has Cecily wakened or asked for me?"

"Uh-uh." Her uncle glanced curiously at her guest, then rose with difficulty from his chair. He reached for his cane. "The little darlin' hasn't made a twitch. Hiya, Ethan."

"Do you mind if Ethan and I talk for a while?" Lisa asked.

"Hello there, Fred," greeted Ethan, taking in at a glance the small room with its worn-down furniture. "Sorry to invade your space. We could go have coffee somewhere if it bothers you."

"Nah." Fred glanced at Lisa with speculation. "Nothing bothers me once I get to sleep. I guess I'll go on to bed, if you don't mind. My bones don't rest as good as they used to settin' up. Nice to see you, Ethan."

They watched the old man limp out of the room, leaning heavily on his cane. Lisa shed her coat, then took Ethan's. "Do you want some coffee?" she offered.

"Nope. Don't want anything," he said, sinking to the corner of the old sofa as she laid the coats on the chair Fred had vacated. His glance demanded more.

"Okay then. I guess perhaps...I think... wait here." She bit down on her bottom lip. "I want to show you something."

Twenty minutes ticked away with the speed of a snail. Restless, Ethan tapped his fingers against his crossed knee. Then he heard a slight shuffling, and Lisa strolled back into the room.

A Lisa he'd never seen before.

She was a totally different woman—a working girl, for sure. The thought drifted through Ethan's mind with stunning speed.

She stood with one hip thrust out, her fist resting on it. The blouse she wore had a deeply rounded neckline, revealing interesting cleavage. Lots of it. The dark-red material stopped short at her waist, showing the white skin of her midriff. Her skimpy black skirt ended at mid-thigh, revealing long silky legs, and on her feet were black spike-heeled sandals.

Her lips, painted a dark shade of red, parted, and she batted lashes thickened with heavy mascara. Her hair was fluffed to stand high on her head, making her look taller. Earrings, five of them, lined her left ear.

Ethan felt as if the floor had opened and he'd fallen through it. He gaped at her. This woman was *Lisa?*

He said the first thing that came to mind. "What are you dressed like a call girl for?"

Then, seeing the pain in her eyes, he immediately regretted his words. Why had he said that? His shock must have numbed his brain. "Sorry… But what are you trying to prove?"

He couldn't help himself. His gaze traveled slowly up and down her body. He'd known women who dressed like this, but never on a professional level, only through his work as a professional banker.

No doubt about it. Her body looked luscious. He swallowed hard. He thought she fought tears, and was sorry he'd sounded cruel.

She lifted her chin. Her lips trembled. "I've never been a call girl, Ethan, but…I partied." She glanced down at herself, tugging on her skirt. "Don't know why I kept these clothes, but they're going in the Goodwill bag after tonight."

She sighed. "When I didn't have a regular boyfriend, I went to every hot spot in town. To dance. To meet men. I danced till morning sometimes. Over the years I knew all the popular disc jockeys and band members by their first names. But I never went home with any of them, I—"

Raising her hand, she tried to swipe the tears from her eyes and stared across the room. The anguish in her eyes stabbed Ethan in the heart. Her voice husky, she said, "I've given all that up now. That life…."

She turned back to look at him, and the movement was almost seductive.

His mouth was dry. He wanted to move, but he remained still—in his place. He didn't know what to say and mumbled, "Why are you telling me this? I can't believe…I guess I can't equate who you are in New Beginnings with…with this image."

A slight smile broke the tension. She kicked off her sandals and curled up at the opposite end of the sagging sofa, tucking her feet under her.

"I'm glad of that. So very glad. I don't want to be this person anymore. But I wanted you to see who I was, what my life was like. I guess I want you to know what you're letting yourself in for if you help me."

Lisa turned to face him. She bit her lip.

"Do you recall the story in the papers about the Donoto Real Estate scam?"

"Ah…" He threw back his head and closed his eyes. He needed the brief respite; his mind was in a whirl. "Yeah, a bit. The guy was skimming off the money as fast as investors gave it to him, wasn't he? He left the investors with blank certificates that weren't worth the ink they were written with, if I remember correctly."

She nodded. "Yes, that's the one. Do you recall there was a woman involved? A girl in his office who signed those certificates…or some of them anyway."

He opened his eyes and studied her face. Lines of pain radiated from her eyes and mouth.

"You?" he guessed shrewdly.

"Yes. Me."

"You're *that* woman? But her name was…Lorie something?"

"Yes."

"But she went to prison!"

"Yes. Lorie Lisa Marley. I went to prison for eighteen months for my part in that scheme. When Beth Anne came there and started the Bible Study, I wanted nothing to do with it at first. I had an attitude about do-gooders, knowing people like Aunt Katherine and all."

She began to pluck at the end of her skirt, pulling it as far down over her bare legs as possible.

"But Beth Anne…she was…oh, I guess… not sweet, exactly, but straightforward and down to earth. And real. She didn't play games, and that impressed me. She gave us hope. And challenged us to read Scripture. I was caught up in them, and over the months of the Bible Study, I came to believe in it all in spite of myself. I didn't want to. But I began to think of God as a reality, as a father, and I'd never had a father. And Jesus as…oh, my savior, yes, but as a big brother, too. Someone who cared about me."

"You found your faith."

She nodded. "Uh-huh. I found a faith so positive that—that I began to think differently about my life. You see, I want to be a real mother to my little girl. She's all I'll ever have. She deserves a real mom, don't you think?"

"Yeah, she does." He was silent a moment. "And the man? What was his name?"

"Rudy Kanner. He's Cecily's father."

"Ah…" A feeling of jealousy threatened to invade him, but he suppressed it. Her life before…it didn't matter now. The compassion he felt overrode any misgivings. Besides, Lisa in a talkative mood was not to be denied.

"That's my problem, Ethan. It's just that I've become so angry...how could a person do such a thing? I have this overwhelming need for revenge. I want to see that man pay for skimming those investments and letting me take the blame. I'd like to hang him up by his—"

She bit down so hard he could hear her teeth grinding. "Well, you know what I mean. I want him to be three times as miserable as he's made me."

Something from the long-ago newspaper report nagged at him. "But didn't he leave the country?"

"Yep, he sure did."

She got up and paced to the door, gazing out the window at the cold night. She shivered, and murmured low, as though talking to herself, "I can't believe how dumb I was. At my age, too. Women sometimes believe the stupidest lies. Lies they've also told themselves maybe. But I swear, he was so persuasive and charming at first...he could have charmed the birds from the trees."

"I've known guys like that." And naive women like Lisa, he thought.

"He told me his wife was sick, and he needed to hospitalize her. He told me his marriage hadn't been a real marriage for years, and that she was about to die."

He stared at her bare feet, toes curled. They made her look vulnerable.

"I knew it was wrong, but he said he'd pay the money back when her insurance kicked in and it would happen before anyone caught on. He told me he wanted to marry me."

She sighed.

"What happened then?"

"I found out I was pregnant. That blew it. I don't know why it shocked him more than it did me, but it did. We argued. Said I should get rid of the thing. He called it a *thing!* I was so furious, he couldn't even call…it was *a baby!*

"We barely spoke for a while, then one day he told me he had a surprise for me, and I got into his car without a single suspicion. Dumb me, I thought it was a trip to my favorite restaurant. It turned out to be an abortion clinic."

"What did you do?"

"I panicked."

"And?"

"I couldn't even get out of the car. While we were talking about it—fighting, really— I saw a girl come out. With her mother, I presume. She couldn't have been more than fifteen. Anyway, her face was white as paper, and she didn't look very happy. I felt sick. After that, I refused even to go into the building. Rudy became so angry, he was rabid. Raving and screaming. It opened my eyes. I'd never seen him that way before.

"Anyway, I quit my job then and there. Rudy scared me so much, I simply didn't go in to work the next day. When he called, I told him I was ill. But he bugged me about those papers he'd had me sign. They were put away in the safe, so I told him that.

"He insisted I come into the office. I made an excuse not to, but he said that was okay because he'd bring them to me, at the apartment."

"What did you do then?"

"I got out. I left the apartment and went to the mall."

"But Rudy caught up with you sometime, didn't he?"

"Yeah, a couple of days later. I didn't

know he was in the office—his car wasn't there. I went late, when I thought the office was closed. I figured I could sneak in to pick up my things."

"What did you have there that was so valuable?"

She laughed ruefully. "Nothing. But I thought differently at the time. Rudy was waiting, and he had those papers for me to sign. I did it, I signed the papers. All the time I knew it was wrong, but I only wanted to get out of there, and I wanted nothing more to do with Rudy. It was only later that I learned he was on the point of being arrested, and he'd left the country."

"How did you find out?"

Lisa sighed. "I got caught. Detectives came to my apartment. It was all downhill from there."

She was silent then. Her face was tight, and she stood with her hands wrapped around her.

"I was in prison for eighteen months. I had to sell everything I owned, trying to pay back some of the money, but it was a pittance compared to what was stolen. And I hired a lawyer. I didn't want a court-appointed one. Foolish of me, but there it is."

"Thank God for Beth Anne," he muttered, thinking of all the dreadful things that could have followed. He'd heard many horror stories of what happened to people in prison. Thank God Beth Anne found her…

"Mm-hmm. Don't think I haven't." She spoke in a quiet, intense tone. "And I thank God for my salvation, as well. My life is so different now. But I can't get the idea of finding Rudy out of my system. He needs to pay!"

"Lisa, you've got to let it go. Let the police handle it, that's what they do."

"I know, I know. But I think I can discover where Rudy is, see? I know his Internet habits, and when I can, I watch those chat sites that he likes."

"Where? On whose computer?"

"The library has lots of computers now. I go whenever I can. Uncle Fred had been picking me up at night."

A thin wail came from the bedroom. Instantly, Lisa was up.

"I'll be right back," she said.

"That's all right, Lisa. I have to go."

"You'll keep what I've told you quiet, won't you, Ethan? I wouldn't want the New Beginnings crowd to think I do nothing but cheat…"

"Of course. But tomorrow…"

"Mommy?"

"We'll talk further tomorrow," he said. He leaned to place a quick kiss on her cheek, then hurried out the door.

Ethan drove home at a slow pace. Astounded at what Lisa had revealed, he had to process it all. At New Beginnings, she was so different; she was rather quiet and reserved. But Beth Anne knew of Lisa's background, and he'd bet his bottom dollar Michael did, too.

No doubt about it, Lisa was struggling to change. To find a new life. He appreciated all that she'd done so far. He'd like to steer her clear of trying to find Rudy, though. But…if he could only help her, maybe she could forget about Rudy entirely. Revenge didn't usually pay off.

Still, he thought he'd go see Michael tomorrow. He would know how to handle this situation.

He only wished he didn't feel…oh… rather knocked out by the knowledge of Lisa's past. It felt strange, especially now that he had to admit to himself he was in love with her.

How long had *that* been true?

For the first time in a while, he prayed from deep within himself. He prayed without thinking about it, prayed simply as the words came.

*Oh, Lord...this is the first day of the rest of my life. I've got three kids to think about, and I...I'm in love with Lisa. I don't know what to do or how to handle this situation. I think I'm in over my head. Help me, don't let me be bowled over by this.*

A flash of memory came to him—Lisa's look of deep pain—and he felt a sorrow for all the sad experiences she must have gone through and life events that had proved empty for her. By the time he pulled into his garage, he'd made up his mind. Over his head or not, he would help her as much as he could.

As for the emotion called love...he'd just let it rest for a while... He'd deal with that later.

## Chapter Sixteen

Ethan slept poorly that night, worrying over Lisa. The knowledge that he loved the woman played at the edges of his mind. She'd faced some serious charges, and come through. But now her struggles appeared to be more than she could cope with.

What was she trying to do? He'd played it cool while he'd been with her, allowing little surprise to show after his first outburst, but the more he thought about her situation, the more concerned he became.

That first outburst shamed him now.

Making oatmeal the next morning, he responded to his children's conversation absentmindedly. Jordan watched television in his pajamas.

"Can we have macaroni and cheese for supper?" asked Bethany.

"Uh-huh. Will do," he answered absently.

What would Lisa do now? How *should* she handle all these problems? Wonder what Mike Faraday thought of it all? he mused.

"Dad, I can't get my Playskool in my backpack," said Tony.

"Hmn.... You've got too much stuff in it. You can't take your Playskool with you anyway."

"I know, but I don't want Jordan to get into it."

"Put it up on the bookshelves in my room. Jordan can't get to it there." He hurried his kids out to catch the bus.

As soon as Bethany and Tony were on their way, he punched in Michael's number. A phone call would suffice for now, with all he had to do. After a stumbling start, he told Michael about the scene at the restaurant, about Lisa getting fired, and the late-night conversation he'd had with her.

"I suppose you know all about Lisa. Her...background and all?"

"Yeah, Ethan, I know," Michael said softly. "But we have to give her a break. That's what we do in New Beginnings, isn't it? Lisa needs our ministry as much or more than anyone I know. And she's trying so hard. She's shown a real passion for decency since her prison term."

"Yes, but she's hit a patch of despair, and I wondered if there was anything we could do to help."

"Hmm… She's the very kind of person we started New Beginnings for in the first place. It's for people who need change. People who need our Lord's forgiveness. Sometimes people need a little help in finding that change, though."

"I know, I know." Ethan rubbed the back of his neck. He was fighting a nagging headache. "I don't think I did understand the ministry clearly before, but I do now. But I don't think Lisa has forgiven *herself*… And Lisa can't go on staying with her uncle Fred. There isn't enough room, for one thing. And she doesn't have a sitter, no one to keep an eye on Cecily while she looks for work."

"What about you two trading time?" Michael said. "You watch Cecily along with Jordan while she works, then she can watch your children. Wouldn't that help?"

"That would be okay sometimes, I suppose, but not often enough. Besides, I—

she's doing some work for me. She's really good, y'know? She catches all the small things with the construction people. And besides, I'm so close to opening. Another month."

Realizing how selfish that sounded, Ethan caught his breath with a groan. Rats! He'd been a selfish beast!

He brushed his fingers through his hair, his hand ending at the back of his neck. He massaged the area. "Guess I'll have to figure out something. Though willing, her uncle Fred is past the point where he can look after a child. He can barely get around."

"Yeah, I noticed at Christmas. Tell you what—I'll make another call on Lisa's aunt Katherine. See if I can soften her up some— maybe she can help on a part-time basis. She wasn't receptive the last time, but perhaps she'll be now. Can't hurt anyway."

"Okay. That'll be good. Hey, I gotta run." Jordan was tugging on his pant leg. "Let me know how you fare."

"Daddy, I want some cereal," Jordan pleaded. His third child was used to being put off, Ethan realized. He needed to listen more carefully.

"Sure, tiger."

After he'd gotten some cereal from the cupboard, he poured some in a bowl and handed it to Jordan. "You can eat it in front of the TV today."

"Yaaay!" Jordan was excited at the unusual privilege.

Ethan settled down to make a call to his sister. He wanted that car today.

Lisa would have to find a reliable day care situation, but that would take time. And selfishly, he realized he'd come to count on her help in opening his restaurant. If he officially employed her, he'd start paying her a real salary.

The restaurant needed her, he reasoned.

Only the restaurant? He was honest enough to admit *he* needed Lisa.

He couldn't sort out all the emotions stirring inside him, but he did know Lisa was important to him. It shocked him a bit to realize just how much he wanted her to be a part of his life, his family. Lisa and Cecily.

He pushed those thoughts aside. He had enough to balance at the moment.

But this guy she'd been mixed up with…Rudy something. Was it usual for a person to crave revenge as Lisa did? Had the hurt she'd suffered forever stamped her?

Not if he had anything to do with it!

She'd been searching the library computers… Was that reasonable behavior? Granted, she wanted justice, but revenge?

Justice…

That was it! What she called revenge, he called justice. The word riveted his attention. He needed to discuss this with Michael, he thought.

There was a lawyer within the New Beginnings group. What kind of law William Llewellyn practiced, Ethan couldn't say. But it was a start. It might be a good idea to consult with him.

Feeling slightly better to be taking action, Ethan punched in the numbers to Fred's house.


Lisa sat at the tiny breakfast table, glumly sipping coffee while she read the want ads in the paper. Her life had taken another wild turn. Ethan was probably lost to her, thinking her nutty. Or criminal.

Why wouldn't he? Why had she thought it important to show Ethan how she used to dress? She hadn't worn those clothes for years. She didn't even know why she'd kept them; she'd had to search for them in a box beneath the bed.

Cecily swung her leg, kicking the chair while munching on her toast, talking to the dog. Endure sat begging, but Lisa paid little mind. She heard Uncle Fred shuffling about in his room, preparing to join them.

Lisa sighed. Maybe she was turning into her mother, but she thought she'd cling to her new modesty. How could she teach her daughter right from wrong if she didn't practice it?

Nobody had told her that changing her life would be easy, and she admitted there were days she found it very difficult. But the New Beginnings ministry was good to her. Besides, she no longer had the desire to head out to clubs and dance the night away, or even to search out old friends.

She was a mom now, and she'd be content to act like a sane, responsible one.

But how could she look for a job until she had Cecily settled? Flipping the paper, she started reading day care ads.

The phone rang. Glancing up, she bit her lip. Who was it, so early in the morning?

She heard Fred answer. "Yeah, she's here, but—" He called her to the phone.

"Lisa?" Ethan sounded short of breath.

"Yes?" She caught hers. Ethan was

calling her? He hadn't been totally turned off by her story last night? He hadn't thought his children would be…smeared, somehow?

He was rushing to give her instructions.

"I'll be by to pick you up at ten, so don't take off anywhere, okay? We can pick up my sister's car this morning. I'll have Jordan with me, so you can bring Cecily."

He didn't say a word about last night, about what she'd told him. Didn't he believe her? Or didn't it affect him?

"You really mean it? You're getting me a car?" She let her breath out, flabbergasted.

Or didn't her past matter to him?

"I can't expect you to do all this running for me any longer without your own car, can I? And you're doing a fantastic job, Lisa. I hope you'll continue."

"Really?" Her voice sounded high-pitched as she felt all her muscles let go. Relief flooded through her and she smiled broadly at Uncle Fred and Cecily. Ethan had said she was doing a fantastic job.

Tears threatened as she hung up the phone. Ethan was giving her another chance. He believed in her, that she wanted a fresh start.

"You want to help me feed Endure some

dog food?" Fred asked Cecily. Her daughter nodded.

"You'll have to be quick, Uncle Fred. Cecily and I have a date."

"Well, now…"

As he'd promised, Ethan pulled into the drive at ten and honked. Lisa waved to him from the door, then appeared a few minutes later, holding Cecily's hand. Jordan sat in the back seat in his car seat.

"I don't have a car seat for Cecily," Lisa muttered. Why hadn't she thought to ask for it?

She wouldn't be beholden to Aunt Katherine for one more thing, that's why. But she let it go.

"It's all right. Here we go, Cecily." Ethan lifted the little girl. "We'll buckle her in tightly, then go buy one first thing."

"Okay." Lisa felt wide-eyed. "I guess that'll work."

"And there'll be no more library computers," he said as she tucked her daughter in beside Jordan.

"What's that?" she asked, climbing into the passenger seat.

"You can use my laptop. I seldom need it,

so you can hang on to it until the restaurant is complete."

"That's great. I had used—" She stopped as a thought hit her. "Oh, my goodness…I have a laptop, I think. It's in storage along with the other office equipment. Rudy accidentally left it when he took off. Why didn't I remember it before? I think I still have the key."

"You have access to office equipment?"

"Yeah, I do. It's not mine, of course, but it belongs to Donoto Real Estate. When Rudy opted to leave, he left instructions to put everything in storage, and I did. I told the police at the time, but as far as I know, they didn't do anything with it after they searched the site."

"And you think a laptop is in there?"

"Well, it was the last time I looked, which was well over two years ago since the equipment was in storage. I don't think Rudy intended to leave it behind, but once he did, he couldn't come back for it."

"Could there be anything on it that would tell you where Rudy went?"

"No, I don't think so…" She frowned. "Maybe. I recall Rudy being somewhat nervous the last day, and he rushed me off my feet with things to do while he cleared out the safe where he kept the money. I didn't know that, of course. I thought he was crazy with worry over the hospitalization of his wife."

She glanced into the back seat. The kids giggled with each other. Nevertheless, she lowered her voice.

"I didn't know it was the last time I'd ever see him. But Cecily had a cold that morning, and my mind was on her. But he said...he told me he was going out of town to open at a new location. Only later did I find out the new place was a sham. I just called the moving people and had them take all the stuff to a storage site, paid them for a year out of petty cash, and forgot about it. Wonder what happened to all that stuff?"

"I don't know, you can call the storage people."

"I will. Right away. I was surprised when I went into Rudy's office and found the laptop. I was going to take it home with me, I think, but in the excitement..."

She thought a moment. "You know, I think I did take it. It was packed in a box..."

"Where is your stuff now?"

"Would you believe in Aunt Katherine's basement?"

He groaned aloud. "Will she let you get it?"

"I hope so. She didn't really want me to leave it, but I had no money for storage, and Uncle Mark convinced her to let me."

The children shrieked with laughter, and she turned to quiet them. They took time to run into a busy mall and found a car seat for Cecily.

"I don't expect the child to use it for more than another year," Lisa explained as she paid the cashier. "But I want her to be safe while she's with me."

They arrived at a large house in Lee's Summit. Ethan urged her to get out of the car as she sat taking in the long white porch and elegant door. "C'mon, this might take a while."

They exited the car and pulled the kids from the back seat. Lisa walked slowly behind Ethan, while the kids ran up the walk. This was Ethan's sister's house, and she didn't know how Stacy would accept her.

Ethan rang the bell, then opened the unlocked door. "Stacy? I'm here. Is the car in the garage?"

A tall woman who looked much like Ethan appeared, and Jordan threw himself at her knees.

"Hiya, pumpkin." She glanced up from messing the child's hair. "Yes it is. I'm so glad to get rid of the thing. Now I can get my new car. Oh…hello. I didn't know you were bringing someone."

"Where's Jessie and Doyle?" asked Jordan.

"They're at school, hon," Stacy answered while gazing curiously at Lisa.

Ethan made hurried introductions.

"Oh, yes. I've heard all about you." Stacy brushed her chin-length hair behind one ear. "You're the one helping Ethan with his restaurant, aren't you?"

Lisa shyly admitted she was. Did Stacy know *all* about her? She doubted it. Her expression was kindly enough.

"Let's go, sis. Don't want to waste any time."

They went outside and around the house. Stacy raised the garage door to reveal a dark-green midsize car.

"Still runs," Stacy said. "I just want a new one."

What was it like to merely *want* a car, then to fulfill that desire? Lisa mused. She'd worked hard and extra hours to buy a used one a few years back.

"Here you go, Stacy," Ethan said, pulling a check from his pocket and handing it to her. "Can we take it now?"

"Sure, but what's your rush?"

"Keys?"

Making a sound of disgust, Stacy handed the keys over. "Don't you want some tea or something?"

"We'll stay another time," Ethan said, in turn handing the keys to Lisa. "But we've got things to do now. Gotta register the car, and I've got a rehearsal soon."

"Oh, that. All right. Nice to meet you, Lisa."

Lisa nodded. "Thanks. Thanks a lot." She blinked fiercely to keep the tears back. "You don't know how much I appreciate this. I—"

"It's okay, Lisa." Ethan took the brand-new car seat out of his vehicle and buckled it into the green one. "Stacy's glad to get rid of it. She's been dying to trade it in for a new SUV."

After strapping Cecily in her car seat, Lisa climbed in herself. She couldn't believe she had a car. A green sedan about five years old. It started at the first turn of the key.

"You owe me a nice long visit, Lisa," Stacy remarked, sliding a glance Ethan's way. "Ethan seldom tells me anything I really want to know."

"Uh-uh, you'd blab to Mom and Dad, down in Arizona."

In her rearview mirror, Lisa saw Ethan laugh. It was the laughter of understanding between close siblings. These two understood each other very well, Lisa thought. She stared with envy. She'd longed for that kind of close relationship when she was a girl.

It was never to be, but at least she had Uncle Fred now. And of course Cecily. She turned to look over her shoulder, gazing at her daughter.

This was her legacy to the world…and she loved the little girl with all her being. She'd do everything in her power to raise her child well by being a responsible, well-adjusted mother.

Heaven only knew she was working on it! But heaven would have to give her more help.

## Chapter Seventeen

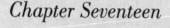

They drove in tandem back to the restaurant location. The street appeared busier today, with activity at the art gallery down the street. After doing a quick inspection of the construction, Ethan glanced at his watch. "I've got to go. Going to be late for rehearsal."

"Can Jordan stay with me and Cecily?" Lisa asked.

His eyebrows rose. "Sure you want him? He can be a handful at times. But he'd enjoy staying with you more than hanging out with the musicians."

"Yes, I think it's a rather good idea." Lisa glanced at the children. They were running in a circle in the middle of what would one day be the dining area and with the tables and chairs Ethan had chosen with her help. "The kids get along well. What time will you be through with rehearsal?"

"About noon. I have to be home for Tony's arrival from school."

"Why don't I be there for Tony? Then you can do your extra errands after rehearsal. You can also talk to the meat supplier."

"Hey, great! That'll work just fine. Here, Jordan," he stooped to Jordan's level. "I'm going to leave you with Cecily and Lisa, okay? Gotta go to work. I'll see you later."

"'Kay."

"Gotta switch the seat," Ethan mumbled, and he leaned into the car and removed Jordan's seat, placing it into the green car.

"Seems to be a lot of bother—playing car seat shuffle," Lisa said apologetically.

"Nah." Ethan pulled his key ring from his pocket and removed a key, then handed it to her. "Only a little extra exercise. What are you going to do now?"

She called the two children to get into the car and settled them into the seats. They giggled at what only they understood.

"We'll be at the library for an hour or so…"

On the way to his own car, he stopped short and turned back. "Lisa, don't… ."

His expression held leashed anxiety. For her?

"Have to. Don't you see? I have to keep trying." Her voice held a restrained anguish. She cleared her throat, then remarked lightly, "Besides, the library has story time about now. If we hurry, we can make it. "

"What about that stuff you took from the real estate office? You might find something in that."

She sighed. "I haven't gotten it. I guess I don't feel like wrangling with Aunt Katherine again just yet."

"Okay, that's the morning then." He wasn't happy about her plans, but he got into his car, still talking. "Feed the kids, please. They'll be hungry long before I get home. You'll find stuff in the fridge. Why don't you wait to eat with me?"

He was making a date?

"Then we'll see about tackling Aunt Katherine together."

Taken aback, she blinked. He wanted her to wait for him to share a meal. He supported her? With Aunt Katherine, even.

All of those realizations hit her at once. He trusted her completely….

Not knowing what to say, she replied automatically. "Sure. Will do. But you have to be at work by three."

"Hmm…yeah." A flash of amusement sparked from his eyes and he looked down at the ground a moment. "I'll have to see about that later. Seems to me there's enough to do here now, and I no longer have the time to work for anyone but myself."

Shock drained her ability to speak. He was going to quit his job? In sympathy? For her? In a lifetime, no one had ever done such a thing.

Her emotions were awhirl, her thoughts scattered this way and that. She almost missed what he said next.

"Maybe we can go over the menus this afternoon. Make the final selections, then get them to the printers."

Printers? She grabbed sanity and held on to it for all she was worth.

"Oh, that's a good idea," she nearly gushed. She nodded in agreement before he had a chance to change his mind. "Will do."

All the feelings of failure seeped away. He trusted her. For the first time since she'd had the run-in with Marie at the restaurant, she felt lighthearted. "There's lots to do for the opening."

*He trusted her!*

Her confidence rose as high as the treetops.

He trusted her and she wouldn't let him down. She knew she could take care of all the multitasking that the restaurant needed. She was good at that.

She spoke to the children as Ethan left, telling them about the story time at the library. "You'll be good and listen to the story, won't you?"

They both nodded. She felt thrilled to be driving a decent car. It was for her use, Ethan had said. He trusted her.

At the library, she made sure the children had chairs in the storytelling circle, then eased over to the computers. She searched the usual Web sites, and glanced at a couple of new ones, all the while keeping an ear trained on the children.

But her search was in vain… She sighed her frustration. Rudy had to be somewhere.

The story circle was breaking up. She smiled and thanked the storyteller, then packed the kids into the car and drove to Ethan's home. It seemed strange to enter his house without him there. The house cried out Ethan.

She wondered what it would be like to share a house with a man…a man who was a husband, a lover…a man like Ethan. To see his things lying about the house, she thought as she picked up a cup that held the remains of his coffee.

But she was there on business. She shouldn't…wouldn't let it feel weird, or let her imagination run away with her. There was enough to do while she waited.

Ethan breezed through the back door into the kitchen a couple of hours later. She put her finger to her lips, indicating the need for silence. The two little ones were asleep on either end of the couch, while Tony quietly watched television.

"Wow, what did you do in here?" Ethan asked, gazing about the large kitchen-family room. It looked wonderfully neater than when he'd left it.

"Oh, picking up toys and things wasn't any bother, was it, Tony?" She'd rather enjoyed the task, and by enlisting Tony's help, she'd come to know him a little better.

"Uh-uh." Tony turned to rise from his place on the floor. "Hi, Dad. Can we go out for dinner?"

As Ethan talked with his oldest son, she

set napkins at two places on the breakfast bar, then filled glasses with water.

"Dinner already? It's almost two. Haven't you eaten lunch?"

"Yeah, but I want a hamburger."

Ethan raised his brows. "Well, why not? I haven't had an evening meal with my children since I started work at the Blue Bird Café. And there may not be much time in the future with restaurant hours to consider. Sure, son. We'll go for burgers, tonight. All of us."

Did that mean her and Cecily? Lisa wondered. Her heart unexpectedly lifted. Judging by his glance at her, apparently it did. She'd best call Uncle Fred to tell him all was well. She set two salad bowls on the counter.

Ethan leaned toward her and said, "If we show up at Aunt Katherine's house with all the kids, will it make a muddle?"

She bit her lip, doubt in her gaze. "Yes, it might. Aunt Katherine becomes upset with too many children around. That's one reason I wanted Cecily out from under her thumb. She was likely to turn into a robot under Aunt Katherine."

"But the old lady isn't likely to make a

fuss in front of all of us, is she? Not if all you're after is a box from the basement. I can talk to her while you go get it. We can be in and out in five minutes. Won't she want you to get it and be gone, along with four very lively children?"

Lisa gazed at him in amazement! "That's brilliant! That might just work."

"We'll go just before supper when the kids are restless."

"That's…that's positively…Machiavellian!"

"Uh-huh. But if it works…"

"How was rehearsal?" She changed the subject. But she couldn't keep her smile down.

"Awesome! We hadn't had one for a couple of weeks, and we needed it. But the music is coming right along."

"That's nice."

"It's more than nice. My place will draw lots of people, I'm thinking."

Later that afternoon, when they drove to Aunt Katherine's, Ethan's plan worked like a charm. Katherine's happiness at seeing Cecily was undermined by her attempt to keep all the children in one spot. They stood in a tiny knot at the entrance of the living room.

"Aunt Katherine, I'd like you to meet Ethan Vale. I'm working for him now. He's going to have a restaurant close to Independence Square soon."

"Nice to meet you," Aunt Katherine said, her doubtful glance indicating she didn't know whether to believe Lisa or not.

Cecily broke free and trotted to her old room, with Jordan, Tony and Bethany following.

"Here, here, you can't go in there," Aunt Katherine turned after them.

"I want my 'jamas," Cecily said, rummaging in her drawer.

"You can't take them."

"And my baby doll…"

"Those things stay here. You can't have them."

"I've got to get some boxes from the basement," Lisa hurriedly told her uncle.

Lisa heard her aunt's voice fading as she hurried past Uncle Mark and down the back stairs. She hesitated a moment, staring at the very tidy basement; tools against one wall, brooms and dustpan in the corner, a shelving unit full of uniform boxes.

That was the place. She headed toward it.

She ran a glance down the labels; Blue-Flowered Dishes was written on one; IRS Returns on another; Bills, 1995-96 on the next. She didn't have to wonder—she knew that inside those sturdy boxes were financial records for at least the previous twenty years. Aunt Katherine was thorough.

But off to the left on the bottom shelf she found what she wanted. The two boxes she'd left, marked Lisa's Stuff. Lisa pulled them out. The tape remained from three years ago

"Lord, bless Aunt Katherine for that…" she mumbled aloud. Aunt Katherine's strict rules of correct behavior wouldn't let her nose about in someone else's boxes.

A heavy thump from above distracted her. What was going on?

Then she heard Aunt Katherine's voice, loud and angry. One of the children started to cry. Through the noise, Lisa couldn't tell what was happening, but she could imagine.

She picked up the two large containers. They were heavy, and she recalled the difficulty she'd had getting them down there. She struggled up the stairs, almost dropping them, before Uncle Mark took the top one from her.

"Thanks, Uncle Mark."

"My pleasure," he said with a conspiratorial grin.

Jordan, great tears streaming down his face, clung to his father's neck. The other children were jumping around him.

"Can you not keep your children quiet?" Aunt Katherine practically screamed. "I never saw such behavior. There's no need for all this." Her aunt gave Lisa a glance that could kill.

"I'm so sorry to disturb you, Aunt Katherine," she said. "But I have what I need. Come, Cecily. Do you have your pajamas?"

"Uh-huh. See you, Aunt Kat'rine."

Lisa felt a stitch of pity. "Can you give Aunt Katherine a hug? And Uncle Mark? And say thank you?"

Aunt Katherine stiffened, and threw Lisa a glance that said she'd die before being a recipient of her compassion. But then Cecily hurried over to her, and the older woman bent to hug the child in spite of herself.

Cecily turned to hug Uncle Mark, who said, "You be a good girl for Mommy now."

"Uh-huh. I will." The little girl ran out to join the other children, who were now playing on the front steps. Ethan waited just beyond the door.

Lisa turned to her aunt and saw that her mouth was quivering.

All of a sudden, the animosity Lisa held melted like hot butter. Her aunt would never change, but she'd given Lisa as much support as she was capable of giving. She'd cared very well for Cecily, given her a home when Lisa couldn't—and Lisa couldn't repay that with a thousand days of thanks.

She lowered her voice. "Thank you, Aunt Katherine. A million times thanks. I hope you won't regret the—the kindness of helping me out over the years. I do appreciate it. It's a gift I can never repay."

Lisa turned to go. Behind her she heard a sob, then Uncle Mark making soothing noises.

I can't just leave...

Shoving the boxes at Ethan, she turned and faced her aunt. Her arms went out to circle both Mark and Katherine, her hands patting their backs. "Bye, Aunt Katherine. Thanks again."

She backed away, then turned and went out the door.

She nodded to Ethan, then glanced once more over her shoulder. She doubted she'd come here again unless specifically invited.

"Okay, gang. Let's go get hamburgers and fries," Ethan said, herding the children into the car.

"I don't think I can wait to get into those boxes," Lisa murmured a short time later, when they were on their way. Her voice sounded almost normal. She appreciated Ethan not talking immediately after they'd left Aunt Katherine's. Jordan sat between them in the front seat. Cecily seemed content in the back with Bethany and Tony.

"I know what you mean. But we can wait another hour, can't we?"

She gave a heavy sigh. "I suppose so. I need to call Uncle Fred, I think. I've been gone the whole day, since early this morning. He'll worry about us."

"Here's my cell phone. Call him. Why don't you tell him to meet us?"

"You wouldn't mind? Really?"

"No. Not at all."

"Okay. While I'm at it, I think I'll call Beth Anne and ask her to meet us later at the church to open up the boxes."

"And Michael?"

"Really? Oh, all right. We might as well have the whole shooting match, I guess."

She made the appropriate phone calls,

keeping them short, then they were at their location.

Uncle Fred showed up at the restaurant soon after they were seated, and the kids hailed him with glee. It truly seemed a party.

After they ate, they drove to the church. A light was on in Michael's office. Beth Anne waited there, as well. Ethan settled his children.

"Okay, now—let's do it," Ethan said.

"Here's hoping…" muttered Lisa.

Slowly, Lisa went to her knees in front of the first box. She thanked Michael as he handed her a letter opener. She stabbed the tape, then ripped it open.

Beth Anne leaned against the desk. "This is a little like opening a hidden treasure, isn't it?"

"It is, but I think I remember what all is in here," Lisa told her. "Files the police didn't want… They took the bigger computers…we had two."

And there it was. A rather small black case. She lifted it from the box, then sat down on the floor and opened it.

"I have no idea if it'll work or not. Three years…"

"Batteries are likely to be dead. I have some if you need them," remarked Michael.

"Let's see…"

It took a moment, as if the long years had slowed down the computer. But it finally lit up. Hurriedly, Lisa typed in a few commands. Nothing.

Holding her disappointment in check, she tried again. Still nothing.

"It's no use," Lisa mumbled. She tried not to let her despair show. "Rudy must've wiped it clean. I just thought…the laptop was always so important to him, I'd hoped it would tell us something. "

"Hmm… Charlie's the guy that can find out what was on it."

"Can he?" asked Ethan. His voice was eager.

"Who is Charlie?" Lisa asked, gazing at Michael, her hope suspended.

"He's a member of New Beginnings," Michael said. "And he can fix most things you'd need on a computer. He might be able to call the information back."

Hope rose up again, and Lisa fought to keep it in check. She'd been disappointed so many times before.

*All right, Lord,* she prayed. *The ball is in Your court now.*

## Chapter Eighteen

Charlie wasn't available until the weekend. Lisa and Ethan kept busy by keeping the contractors on their toes, taking care of the last details. They didn't talk about what the laptop might reveal; they just waited. They attended New Beginnings, and for the first time in a long while, Lisa focused hard on the message. She also went to the Friday night Bible Study. Unexpectedly, she found she could concentrate, and she enjoyed it.

But she didn't say a peep to anyone about how poorly she was sleeping on the broken-down couch, or how she was coping full-time with a three-year-old. Only the dark circles under her eyes told the tale.

Finally, when Ethan remarked about it, she confessed part of the truth. "I'm not anxious about what the laptop will show, though I am excited about the possibilities. It's just that the old couch is so uncomfortable."

"The old couch? Is that what you're sleeping on?"

"Yeah. There's no where else to put me. Hadn't you guessed?"

"No, I hadn't thought about it. Boy, that house really is tiny, isn't it?"

She didn't answer, and turned into the restaurant kitchen. It needed only a few touches now, and she ran her hand along one smooth granite counter. Ethan was expecting the first of two applicants for the chef's job, and they'd hired their third waitress yesterday. The grand opening was around the corner.

"We're going to have to do better for you than that," Ethan remarked absently. A young man entered, gazing about with an inquisitive stare. He was short and slender, looking no more than twenty. Ethan gave a half grin. "Here's my applicant. I'll talk to you later."

"Cecily and Jordan?" Lisa called. "Let's go for a walk to the square. It's a nice day."

She left as Ethan shook the young man's hand, then sat down with him at a table near the front of the restaurant. Lisa needed the walk as much as the children to clear her head. She only wished a nap was automatically included in her day, as it was in theirs.

Imagine, she mused as the two children peered into a shop window. Someone might actually be able to find documents that would prove Rudy's culpability in the real estate scheme. Not that they needed proof; his absence along with the investors' money was proof enough.

Nevertheless, excitement ran through her veins, and the thought of Rudy being made to pay caused her to smile.

That night she and Ethan crowded into Michael Faraday's office, along with Beth Anne and, surprisingly, her husband, Reverend Dennis Hostetter.

"I wouldn't miss this for the world," said Beth Anne with a grin, answering Lisa's unspoken question. She thumbed over her shoulder. "Dennis, either."

Lisa nodded appreciation at her friend.

"I've been looking forward to this myself," remarked Michael. "Mysteries always intrigue me. Where are all your kiddies?"

"My young cousin Georgie Dene is baby-sitting," Ethan answered. "She's in college, so the money comes in handy."

"My Cecily is there, too," Lisa told him.

Charlie Smith came in soon after, carrying a very official-looking black case. He was a large individual, and took up most of the remaining space. He brushed his dark hair from his face, glancing from one to the other. "Hiya, folks. I understand you need some material recovered?"

Lisa only knew Charlie casually, having seen him at New Beginnings. More nervous now that the time was here, she only nodded.

"That we do, Charlie," Michael answered. "It's good of you to help us out."

"No problem. Wasn't doing much at home anyway," Charlie said. He set his case on the floor, then went to his haunches, unsnapping the top. "I've got some software that might do the trick."

They all watched as he took things from his case, opened the laptop, and then started to punch the keys.

"I hear New Beginnings is pulling in about forty or more people now," said Dennis Hostetter offhandedly. He folded his arms and leaned against the desk beside Beth Anne, but his eyes were on Charlie.

Michael rubbed the side of his face. "Yes, we've experienced a bit of growth. I hope we can keep it up."

"Do you need a nursery?"

"No, that doesn't seem to be a problem," Michael replied. "Most of the time, anyway." Then he added in a teasing voice, "Ethan, here, is one of our lagers for children."

"Wasn't my fault we got started late," Ethan informed them. "Sharon was offered her dream job and I couldn't object. Then when we started, it seemed we couldn't stop. I just didn't count on losing her...."

Lisa glanced at Ethan. He seldom spoke of his wife. He did so now with a quiet sadness she'd never heard from him before. Her heart tore at the huskiness in his voice, a rending she thought must be audible. But everyone was watching Charlie.

She'd been utterly selfish in not asking more about Sharon. How had he stood the grief?

Beth Anne chuckled, bringing Lisa's mind back to the moment. "Well, late or not, I'm sure Sharon would think you a fine daddy."

He *was* good with his children, Lisa thought. A fine daddy.

Reverend Hostetter shot Ethan a grin.

"Well, they'll keep you young, that's for sure. I can hardly keep up with our grandchildren's activities. One is in the school band, and the other plays baseball."

"Yeah," Ethan remarked. "It's just that most of our New Beginnings members have children who are older than mine. Now that's not a bad thing necessarily. I'm just not able to do everything they are."

"Bingo!" Charlie broke into their conversation.

"What have you found?" asked Ethan.

"Hmm…a list of people…a copy of an ad. Meant for a newspaper, I guess. But here's something you might be interested in, Lisa."

"What is it?"

"Airline schedules to South America. And inquiries into a couple of hotels in Argentina. A transfer of money… Hmm… Then another inquiry into a Mexican hotel a couple of weeks later."

"You got all that?"

"Yeah."

"I knew it. I just knew it!"

"That's fantastic!" Ethan said. "Now you can take that to the police."

"Can't get hard copies yet," Charlie told him.

"What do you mean?" asked Lisa.

"Can't make a printout. I'll have to take it home, where I have more equipment. I can make you a hard copy then, if you want it."

"Yes!" Lisa felt strongly about that. "I definitely want a hard copy. How long will it take?"

"Oh, I can do it tomorrow, I suppose."

"Tonight?" Lisa bargained. She held her breath.

"Okay, tonight. I'll have it for you by morning."

"Thank You, Lord." The words burst out of Lisa, and she closed her eyes tightly for a moment. Relief flooded her. Knowing where Rudy might have headed would give the police something solid to work with. "Oh, thank You. Thank You."

When Beth Anne chuckled, Lisa realized she'd spoken it aloud. Heat rose in her cheeks. "Sorry," she murmured. "I just am deliriously happy to have something to show to the police."

"I'm happy too, dear," Beth Anne responded, still smiling. "It's a wonderful break for you."

"Well, a big thanks to Charlie, too," said Michael.

"Oh, yes! Thank you, Charlie." Lisa stepped

forward and threw her arms about him, hugging him tight.

"Ooh, this is nice," Charlie murmured, his face alight.

"Well, what about the rest of us," Ethan joked.

"I've already thanked you all…" Lisa said, giving them a round of smiles. "But I can say it a million times over and it wouldn't be enough. Thank you for helping me. I don't know what I'd do without you."

"We do it by God's grace, Lisa," said Michael softly. "That's the only way we operate."

"Amen to that," Beth Anne agreed.

"Yes sir, to God's grace," approved Dennis Hostetter.

Lisa blinked. Though she'd heard the expression many times before, it now sunk deep, and she knew that each step of the way had been directed by God.

*By God's grace…*

She felt humbled in a way she'd never felt before.

The next day, Lisa drove alone to the police station. She'd called to make sure the detective who'd been on her case would be there. But she hadn't wanted anyone with her while she presented her evidence of Rudy's whereabouts.

Nervously, she walked up to the front counter. "I'm to see Detective Robinson?"

"Down that hall, third desk to the right," answered the bored desk sergeant.

Her sneakers made no noise, and she soon stood at his desk.

"Detective Robinson?" Her tone was solemn. She recalled each heavy line in his worn face from almost three years prior. He glanced up.

"Uh, yes." He raised a heavy brow. "You're Miss Marley?"

As if he didn't know, Lisa thought. But she held his gaze, not letting intimidation overwhelm her. His hair was grayer, and he favored his left hand. Curiosity was there, deep in his eyes.

"Yes." She couldn't help it, her tongue flicked out to dampen her dry lips. I can do this…by God's grace.

"You're bringing in information about where that boss of yours can be found, I understand?" His tone wasn't cold exactly, just…disbelieving.

She didn't like "that boss of yours" but she made no objection.

"Yes, that's right. I want Rudy brought back here if possible. And prosecuted. I'm almost through with my parole and I don't want anything hanging over my head ever again."

By God's grace, she would never do anything again that would bring her shame and trouble.

"That's good." He casually flipped a paper aside and sat forward. "Now let's see this evidence."

She lifted the laptop onto his desk. "This is Rudy's laptop. I don't think he intended to leave it behind, and I…that is, the police didn't find anything on it, so they returned it to me."

"Hmm…" His glance sharpened. "What do you want me to do with it? Should have been with the rest of the evidence."

She skipped over that one. The mistakes the police had made were their own.

"Well, I have a friend who's good with computers. Charlie brought back what was there…and here're the hard copies of what he found."

The detective glanced at the papers she

handed him. Then he muttered, "You'd better sit down."

Lisa spent the whole morning explaining the old scam, and how she'd played a part in it. She told him how Rudy had ripped off the money and lied to her to get her to help him, then left her as a front in the real estate office. She told the detective that she had an idea where Rudy and his wife had gone and that she'd tried to trace him. She wanted him to come back and face charges for what he'd done.

*By the grace of God,* she thought. She counted on that.

The detective turned on a recorder, and she had to start her story all over again. For over three hours she talked, and in the end, the desk had five chairs around it as people gathered to listen.

When she finally left the police station, she drove to Ethan's house. She felt exhausted and empty. She wanted to go home and sleep—Uncle Fred's house represented home, at least. He didn't require anything of her.

But her little girl was at Ethan's, playing with his kids, and, thank God, she was safe. Safe and happy. Lisa could barely wait to see Cecily's sweet smiles.

Ethan was waiting for her, too. As soon as she entered his house, he asked, "Well, what happened?"

He came forward to meet her. She tried to straighten her slumping shoulders. She glanced at the children, playing in the middle of the family-room floor.

"Oh, the police were very glad to get the information. They took the computer and my printouts." She laid down her purse, looking at the overstuffed couch with longing. "I guess they'll find out where Rudy is…I don't know if they can extradite him or not."

"Ah, honey, don't be downhearted… They'll do everything they can."

"It's just that I feel so exhausted. As though I've run a hundred miles. Finding where Rudy is has been a driving force for so long…"

"All this has taken a toll on you. You'll feel better later. Come and sit down. You can put it behind you now."

Put it behind her? Could she ever put behind her the fact that she'd signed those papers, causing hundreds of people, many of them elderly, to lose so much money?

She thought not.

"I'll bring you some tea," offered Ethan. "The kids are occupied, and I want to talk to you."

Lisa nodded, sinking into Ethan's comfortable sofa, mentally comparing it with the one she slept on. She longed to lay her head on the sofa pillow and close her eyes. She watched the children as they squabbled over the extensive road they'd built over the floor. Cecily ran her red car behind Bethany's.

"Here it is." Ethan appeared before her with a steaming mug. "Now it's hot…"

"Yes, fine." She took the tea, relaxing further into the couch. Her eyes drifted closed. Perhaps she could take a little nap? Here?

"Lisa."

She glanced up. Ethan stood in front of her with a serious gaze. What was it?

"I think we ought to get married right away. Next week, even."

The tea threatened to slosh over the rim as her hand shook with nerves.

"Oh…sorry." Ethan rescued the mug from her and put it on the end table. Lisa stood and brushed nervously at her navy pants. She hadn't heard right…

"What did you say?" she asked. Her throat felt tight and she could hardly talk.

"Sit down, Lisa. I didn't mean to startle you. I only think it's a natural thing to do. You don't want a big wedding, do you? I thought just a nice, simple ceremony would be good. We have so much to finish right now, I thought if we could get the wedding out of the way, then we could get on with the restaurant."

He talked about having a wedding in the same breath as opening his restaurant? *Their* wedding?

Marriage would be a convenience, certainly, but nothing had been said about love.

It would answer all her problems...

She'd have somewhere to live with space for both her and Cecily. She'd have family...

Cecily would have two brothers and one sister. Her child would have playmates every day, someone to help her at school; they'd go to church together, they'd have meals together.

She would have a husband...

Lisa thought about the changes that would bring. She'd have the needs of four children to balance, children who would lighten her days, give her plenty of reason to both worry and celebrate. She'd have a man with whom to share daily life...a partner, someone who would never leave her. She'd have someone with whom to go to church, someone to share her meals, to share work.

Someone to share her bed...

She bowed her head, her thoughts in a whirl. How could she support a marriage without love? How could he?

But she did love him. Lisa loved Ethan, and the knowledge came as no surprise. She'd realized it for a while. Was that enough? Could she do it? Could she marry him with her track record?

"What about...what about my past?" She asked the question in a whisper, her eyes downcast.

She heard his deep breath. "You've been honest about it, haven't you? There's nothing I don't know, is there?"

"No. You know it all."

"Well...something was said the other night when we were fiddling with the laptop. About God's grace..."

Her glance flew up, and she stared into his eyes. That word...*grace*. Had he felt the same significance in the word that she had? *Grace!*

"I think it's only by the grace of God that any of us are forgiven. We're all damaged in some way. His forgiveness is there for all of us, if we but accept it."

"Yes." She nodded. "I accepted His forgiveness while still in prison, and it's very precious to me. Beth Anne led me to the Lord."

"But have you forgiven yourself?"

Had she? She thought hard about all that she'd gone through. The things she'd done and the flippant attitude she'd had, where having fun was most important. She'd come to Beth Anne's Bible Study expecting nothing, only thinking it as a way to pass the time.

But she'd found something beyond herself. Grace...

"I...I don't know. I...I guess I never have. How could I?"

He nodded. "I thought so. You need to do it, Lisa. I've been thinking of that a lot lately, and asking His forgiveness over my antipathy toward Sharon's parents. After I do, don't have a hard time transferring that forgiveness to myself, either."

"I never thought about it that way."

"Can you now? If you don't, then it makes a lie of all His effort. You have to forgive yourself so that you can go on in life."

"I suppose, I…" She licked her lips, then let her eyes close, and in a near whisper, offered, *"Dear God…Father…I am so sorry for all the ways I offended You. You've given me forgiveness, and I haven't even accepted it completely. I didn't understand. I—I guess I harbored a harsh set of thoughts about myself. About where I've been. But now… with Your Grace, I forgive myself."*

She was quiet a moment, then hastily added, *"And Aunt Katherine."*

Ethan chuckled. Just then she heard the noise of the children, saw Cecily yawn widely, and Jordan tugging on his dad's hand. And she knew her forgiveness was complete.

"What is it?" Ethan asked Jordan.

"Can we have some juice?"

"Certainly. Juice coming up."

Lisa leaned back on the couch and watched as Ethan poured four small paper cups with juice. "Here you go, kids. Last snack till dinnertime."

The enormity of her prayer lingered, pushing her thoughts this way and that. It was true. She'd never forgiven herself. Now that she had, she realized it gave her a new freedom. It was in the air she breathed, in the sunshine that radiated through the windows.

Freedom to love Ethan? To love Bethany, Tony and Jordan as she loved Cecily? To love Aunt Katherine as she loved Uncle Fred?

She already loved Ethan—she just hadn't known how to handle it. She'd had so little of real, honest-to-goodness love in her life.

Ethan returned to her side, chuckling. "Well, that'll keep 'em happy for an hour or so. Now what were we saying?"

Lisa took Ethan's hand, looking at the lines there, at his strong fingers that could play guitar strings, make soup or keep account books. Should she trust him to keep her heart?

"I think I'm going to be as demanding as the kids," she said, sitting up.

"Oh?"

"Yes." She folded her fingers inside his. "For starters, I want you to repeat what you started our conversation with."

"The start of our conversation?" His jaw firmed, as though he had to think about it. All the while his thumb tenderly stroked the back of her hand. "Oh, that was, um, let me see…"

"Stop teasing. I want you to tell me what you said."

He raised her hand to his lips. "I said we should get married soon. I don't want to wait for long."

His lips felt tender, and her breath caught. "And?"

He inspected her hand as she had inspected his, and touched her third finger where a wedding band would shine. "We could do it in the restaurant, when the band will be there. That would be quite an opening, and draw—"

"Nope. I want you to tell me *why* we should marry, besides it being convenient."

His gaze was steady. "Oh, you mean because I love you?"

An earth-shattering trembling began, deep in her middle. He loved her…he truly loved her. "That's it. That's what I want to hear."

"Okay. I love you." He said it casually, but something deep in his eyes told her he wanted to say it with passion, when they were alone to indulge themselves with kisses that reflected their feelings.

Would she accept his love?

"Again?" she whispered.

His breathing became heavier, and he said more slowly, "I love you more each day. You fill my heart to overflowing."

Ethan quit playing with her hand and

pressed her palm to his. He held her gaze, never wanting her to leave. He saw a river of love there, overflowing with tears.

"And?"

"And I'll love you forever and a day. I've never thought of what forever meant. But if it means till we're tottering in old age, then I'll love you till then. I'll love you as my wife with a fierce pride. I'll love you sitting beside me as we worship along with our four children. I'll love you as we sit together at meals, at gatherings like New Beginnings, at parties. I'll love you till the day I leave this planet."

She sighed. His declaration held everything she'd ever hoped for. "I love you, too."

"Is that all?" Ethan grinned. He leaned closer to whisper, "I suppose I'll have to wait till we're alone to gain more—" he glanced at the children, engrossed in their play, "—evidence."

Then closer still, "I want to kiss you till you don't know what time it is, and morning comes too soon."

Lisa actually blushed. He watched the color seep into her cheeks. "That's what I want, too. Soon."

His eyes filled with mischief. "Well, I

think we should call Fred, don't you? He needs to get over here to help celebrate. I have a pot roast to fix big enough for a houseful."

"Yes, we'll give Uncle Fred a call. He'll be very happy. Your sister, too, I suppose. But I don't think we should have the ceremony at the restaurant. We should have it at a New Beginnings meeting so that everyone can see our start to a new life."

Ethan thought about that and became serious once more. "Yes. That's it. Our own New Beginning."

And in spite of the four children, he placed his lips against hers in a promise that meant forever.

\* \* \* \* \*

Dear Reader,

Judging is something we do all the time. In fact, I think it's the rule most often broken. We judge the young by what they wear, their spiked hair and their inappropriately placed rings. In our church, there are several young people who dress like that. But I keep my opinions to myself. For God's love is shining through them, just as He shines through the fashionably dressed young woman sitting next to me. The worship those young people offer is just as acceptable, if done truthfully, as mine. So let us all be more wise, and judge not, lest we be judged.

*Ruth Scofield*

# eHARLEQUIN.com

## The Ultimate Destination for Women's Fiction

### Visit eHarlequin.com's Bookstore today for today's most popular books at great prices.

- An extensive selection of romance books by top authors!
- Choose our convenient "bill me" option. No credit card required.
- New releases, Themed Collections and hard-to-find backlist.
- A sneak peek at upcoming books.
- Check out book excerpts, book summaries and Reader Recommendations from other members and post your own too.
- Find out what everybody's reading in Bestsellers.
- Save BIG with everyday discounts and exclusive online offers!
- Our Category Legend will help you select reading that's exactly right for you!
- Visit our Bargain Outlet often for huge savings and special offers!
- Sweepstakes offers. Enter for your chance to win special prizes, autographed books and more.

### Your purchases are 100% guaranteed—so shop online at www.eHarlequin.com today!